Dear Reader,

I just wanted to tell you how delighted I am that my publisher has decided to reprint so many of my earlier books. Some of them have not been available for a while, and amongst them there are titles that have often been requested.

I can't remember a time when I haven't written, although it was not until my daughter was born that I felt confident enough to attempt to get anything published. With my husband's encouragement, my first book was accepted, and since then there have been over 130 more.

Not that the thrill of having a book published gets any less. I still feel the same excitement when a new manuscript is accepted. But it's you, my readers, to whom I owe so much. Your support—and particularly your letters—give me so much pleasure.

I hope you enjoy this collection of some of my favorite novels.

Anne Mather

Back by Popular Demand

With a phenomenal one hundred and thirty-five books published by Harlequin, Anne Mather is one of the world's most popular romance authors. Harlequin is proud to bring back many of these highly sought-after novels in a special Collector's Edition.

Anne MATHER

COLLECTOR'S EDITION

PALE ORCHID

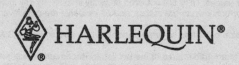

HARLEQUIN®

TORONTO • NEW YORK • LONDON
AMSTERDAM • PARIS • SYDNEY • HAMBURG
STOCKHOLM • ATHENS • TOKYO • MILAN • MADRID
PRAGUE • WARSAW • BUDAPEST • AUCKLAND

ISBN 0-373-63151-0

PALE ORCHID

First North American Publication 1986.

Copyright © 1985 by Anne Mather.

This edition published by arrangement with Harlequin Books S.A.

® and TM are trademarks of the publisher. Trademarks indicated with ® are registered in the United States Patent and Trademark Office, the Canadian Trade Marks Office and in other countries.

Visit us at www.eHarlequin.com

Printed in U.S.A.

CHAPTER ONE

THE WIDE-BODIED JET taxied into its unloading bay, and the extending arm of the disembarking gangway was fitted into position. Across the tarmac, another plane was just taking off, its wings dipping to starboard as it executed the manoeuvre which would take it out across the blue waters of the Pacific, skirting the beach at Waikiki before heading back towards California.

Watching the American Airlines jet climb into the late afternoon sky, Laura Huyton wished, with an urgency bordering on desperation, that she could be aboard that plane, heading back to San Francisco, and on to London. Seven thousand miles was a long way to come to face probable humiliation, and she wondered if she would have set out so confidently if she had known where her quest would lead her.

Most of the other passengers waiting to disembark were holidaymakers, bound for one or other of the many excellent hotels Honolulu boasted. Some, unlike herself, were only stopping off in Oahu, *en route* for other islands in the Hawaiian group, but all of them, it seemed to Laura, were looking forward to their arrival. There had been a definite air of excitement in the aircraft, ever since it left San Francisco, and the stewardesses in their long Polynesian dresses added their own particular colour to the trip.

'This your first visit to Hawaii?' inquired the rather stout matron, who had been sitting beside her all trip, and who had tried on several occasions to engage Laura in conversation—without any success.

'No.'

Laura's response was monosyllabic, but she couldn't help it. She didn't want to talk about Hawaii; she didn't want to be here; and had it not been for a brutal trick of fate, she doubted would ever have come here again.

'You've been before then?' persisted the woman, as the door to the plane was opened and passengers started to block the gangways in their haste to disembark.

'Yes.' Laura slipped the strap of her bag over her shoulder and gathered together the book and magazines she had bought to read on the journey. Then, feeling obliged to say something, if only to get the woman to move out of the aisle seat, she added briefly, 'I used to work here some years ago. It's not a place you forget.'

'Absolutely not,' exclaimed her inquisitor enthusiastically, getting to her feet, and although she would obviously have liked to continue this discussion, she was compelled to move ahead. 'Have a good time,' she added, as Laura slipped into the queue some spaces behind her.

'I intend to.' Laura allowed a small smile that gave her pale features animation. A good time, she reflected ruefully, was the last thing she was likely to have; but that was her problem and no one else's.

The pretty Polynesian girls who waited in the arrivals hall had almost exhausted the supply of flower garlands they handed out to holiday visitors. The *leis*, as they were called, were very popular with tourists, and Laura could still remember her delight when, on her first visit to the islands, she had received the symbolic welcome. Today, however, she sidestepped the smiling throng and hurried on down the escalator, to take her seat on one of the articulated buses, which transported passengers between the arrivals hall and the terminal buildings.

By the time she had collected her luggage from the carousel and summoned a cab, the sun was sinking and, giving the address of the small hotel she remembered, just off Kalakaua Avenue, she settled back to enjoy the ride. Through the open windows of the cab, the air was deliciously warm and pungently familiar. Even before they crossed the Kapalama Canal, she could smell the Dole Canneries, and the water tank, painted to resemble a pineapple, rose like a huge yellow dome, sprouting its prickly stalk.

To her right, the less attractive aspects of the island's economy gave way to the waving masts of the yacht marina. Dozens of sailing craft, from modest dinghies to ocean-going schooners, were moored in the basin, and Laura couldn't help but wonder if Jason still owned his schooner. Not that it had any relevance, she assured herself impatiently, determinedly turning her attention to the exotic elegance of a floating restaurant moored at the quay. How Jason Montefiore might or might not be conducting his private affairs was no concern of hers.

The cab was approaching Kalakaua Avenue, and Laura gazed out at the towering hotel blocks. There seemed more than she remembered, even the 'Pink Palace', as the Royal Hawaiian Hotel used to be called, was overshadowed now by the looming curve of the Sheraton. But the market place was still there, where Jason had once bought her a string of real pearls and the engraved gold medallion, she still carried in her handbag.

Just beyond the imposing towers of the Hyatt Regency, the cab turned into a side street and a hundred yards down, past an intersection, came to a halt outside the modest façade of the Kapulani Reef Hotel. Laura climbed out, dragging her suitcase after her, and handed over the necessary dollars. Thank goodness she had remembered the name of this place, she thought, looking up at its faded exterior. The paint was chipping on the balconies, and the sun had yellowed its colour-washed walls. But so far as she knew, its reputation was still intact, and one of the girls at the agency used to recommend it. Of course, that was more than three years ago now, but it could not be helped. Hotels in Waikiki were expensive, and those Jason had taken her to were quite beyond her means. The Kapulani used to be both clean and reasonable, and she did not have a lot of choice in the matter. Besides, with luck, it might only be for a couple of nights.

She had 'phoned ahead from San Francisco, and she was expected. A polite receptionist had her sign in, and then a Chinese porter was summoned to take her to her room. The lift transported them three floors up to room number 409, and Laura felt obliged to tip the man, even though his manner was anything but friendly. Still, he had carried her suitcase, she reflected, as she took a proper look at her surroundings.

It was clean and neat, she had to admit, the bed one of the wide divans she had become used to during the time she had worked in Honolulu. There was a chest of drawers and a fitted closet, a round glass-topped table and a chair, and the ubiquitous colour television, standing by the open balcony doors. There was also a telephone, the one object Laura most wanted to see, but she put her immediate impulses aside and walked into the adjoining bathroom.

Fifteen minutes later she emerged, considerably cooler and fresher after a shower. Wrapped in a towel, she threw her soiled clothes on to the chair, and then rescued

the key to her suitcase from her handbag and deposited
the case on the bed.

There was a definite disorganisation to the contents of
the suitcase, but it couldn't be helped. For the past three
days, she had thought little about her appearance, and
the garments she had packed with reasonable care in
London, were now muddled beyond belief. That they
were not more creased was due to the resiliency of mod-
ern fabrics, and she drew out the short-sleeved shirt and
pants that were first to hand.

Running a brush through the fine silky hair, that she
generally plaited and wore in a single braid for working
purposes, Laura contained her impatience and walked
out on to the balcony. It was getting dark, but the air
was as soft and velvety as a moth's wing. The temperature stayed balmy most of the time, only becoming hot
and sticky in the summer when the wind called the *kona*
blew. Usually, the climate was perfect, a delicious blend
of sun and trade winds, that made the islands a garden
paradise.

Away to the right, Laura could hear the sound of the
surf, as it creamed along the shoreline, and she was
tempted to leave what she had to do until the morning
and go for a walk along the beach. It would be so nice
to forget her troubles for a while, and enjoy the exotic
beauty of her surroundings. But then, the memory of
Pamela, lying in the hospital in San Francisco, returned
to haunt her, and putting the brush aside, she quickly
threaded her hair into its neat *queue*.

Crossing the room to where the 'phone sat, on the low
bureau beside the bed, Laura reflected that even that image was not as disturbing as the scene which had met
her eyes on her arrival in San Francisco. If she hadn't
responded to Pamela's 'phone call so promptly, if she

hadn't ignored Pierce's complaints about her ingratitude, and taken the first available flight from London, she might never have found her sister alive. As it was, Pamela had been unconscious, the terrible meaning of the empty bottle of sleeping tablets on the table beside her, telling their own tale. Laura shivered, even now. Without her unexpected intervention, Pamela would be dead—and all because of Mike Kazantis.

Before picking up the 'phone, she reached for her bag, and drew out the handful of letters she had found scattered about her sister's body. Without them, she might never have learned the name of the man who had caused her sister so much heartbreak. Pamela could have refused to tell her. Indeed, at first, she had denied any connection between the letters and her attempted suicide. But when the doctors at the Mount Rushmore Hospital had informed Laura that her sister was pregnant, she had immediately understood the situation.

Of course, Mike Kazantis's name would have meant nothing to Pamela. It was less than two years since she had applied for a nursing post in Sausalito, and her work with the elderly, and very rich, Mrs Amy Goldstein, had seemed far removed from the commercial success of Jason Montefiore.

Naturally, after her own experiences in the United States, Laura had tried to persuade her younger sister not to leave England. But short of explaining exactly why she had returned to London, there was little she could say; and besides, it had seemed unlikely that Pamela would make the same mistakes.

Laura shook her head now, and reached for the 'phone. It was not a situation she had ever expected to have to deal with. When she was making her arrangements to accompany Pierce to the Camargue at the be-

ginning of March, Pamela had been writing, saying how
happy she was, and there had been no mention of her
relationship with Jason's brother-in-law. Had she known
he was married? Was that why she had not mentioned
his name to her sister? The little Laura had read of *his*
letters, gave no evidence one way or the other. All that
was clear was that the letters had ceased, approximately
six weeks ago. The most recent postmark was March
14th, and Laura had had no difficulty in making the association.

She rang the club first, guessing that as it was after
six o'clock Jason was most likely to be there. If he was
in Honolulu, of course, she reflected, crossing her fingers. There was no absolute guarantee. Just her own rec-
ollection of his movements, and the fervent hope that
this trip to Hawaii had not been a fool's errand.

A man answered, a man whose voice she didn't
recognise, and adopting her most confident tone, she
asked to speak to Mr Montefiore. 'It's a personal matter
of some urgency,' she explained, hoping that by mentioning the personal nature of her call, the man would
at least be curious.

'Just a minute,' he said, and the line went dead, in-
dicating she assumed that she had been dealt with by a
switchboard, and that her call was receiving more serious attention. *Come on, come on*, she urged impatiently,
running first one, and then a second, moist palm over
the knees of her trousers. Jason wasn't the Pope, after
all. What on earth could be taking so long?

'Yes?'

Another male voice had taken the place of the switchboard attendant, and Laura tried to identify the brusque
address. It wasn't Jason, that much was certain, but there

was something vaguely familiar about that clipped inquiry.

'Oh, hello,' she said again, swallowing her uncertainty. 'I—er—I'd like to speak to Mr Montefiore, please. This—this is Laura Huyton.'

'Laura!' The voice definitely exhibited surprise now, and the warmer vowels gave her her first clue.

'Phil?' she ventured, and hearing his swift intake of breath: 'Phil Logan? Yes, it's me; Laura.' She took a gulp of air. 'Is Jason there?'

'Where are you, Laura?' Without answering, he turned the question against her. 'You sound pretty close. Are you here, in Oahu?'

Laura hesitated, and then she replied resignedly, 'Yes. I arrived a couple of hours ago. Phil, I need to speak to Jason urgently. If he's there, I'd appreciate it if you'd get him to the 'phone.'

There was silence for a few seconds, and then Logan spoke again. 'Does Jason know you're coming?' he inquired, his tone almost imperceptibly cooler now. And at her swift denial, 'What are you doing in Honolulu, Laura? I have to tell you—I don't think Jason will agree to see you.'

Laura's lips compressed. 'What I'm doing here I'll tell Jason, and no one else,' she retorted. 'Don't you think you should at least give him a chance to refuse? It is important. You can tell him that.'

Again the silence stretched between them, and Laura could feel the nerves in her stomach tightening unpleasantly. She had eaten little since that morning, and the hollow feeling she was experiencing was partly due to her emptiness. But, she couldn't deny a certain irritation at the attitude Phil Logan was adopting, and although she knew she had no right to expect anything of Jason, she resented being thwarted by one of his employees.

'I can't ask Jason to speak to you, because he isn't here,' Logan announced at length, and Laura expelled her breath on a sigh.

'You mean—he's at the apartment?'

'Mr Montefiore doesn't live in Honolulu any more, Laura,' he responded reluctantly, his deliberate use of Jason's surname creating a barrier even a fool could not overlook; and Laura was no fool. 'He...er...if you'd like to give me the address of the hotel where you're staying, and your 'phone number, I'll pass your message on. That's the best I can do.'

Laura's jaw quivered, and she clamped her teeth together to arrest the weakness. But it was anger, not emotion, that caused her breathing to quicken and the blood to run more thinly through her veins. How dare Phil Logan behave as if she was some pitiful hanger-on, desperate for a hand-out? she thought furiously. When had she ever treated him with anything less than courtesy, even when she had been living in Jason's luxurious penthouse and Logan had been pulling beers in the nightclub bar?

'Thanks,' she said now, deciding there was no point in pursuing her frustration with him. 'I'm staying at the Kapulani Reef Hotel. It's on Haleiwa Avenue—'

'I know where it is,' responded Logan swiftly, evidently taking it down, and Laura contained her resentment at his tone.

'Room 409,' she added, just for good measure, and then rang off before he could make some comment about her choice of accommodation.

But with the receiver replaced on its cradle, Laura found that she was shaking. Somehow, she had never

expected Jason's employees to treat her like a pariah.
Phil Logan had acted as if Jason had thrown her out,
instead of the way it really was. Was that what Jason
had told his men? That he had thrown her over?

Getting up from the bed, she walked nervously across
to the open windows, rubbing her palms against the unexpectedly chilled flesh of her upper arms. So much for
speaking to Jason tonight, she thought bitterly. He might
not even get the message. If she didn't hear from him
within the next twenty-four hours, she would have to
think of some other method of finding him. But how?
Logan hadn't even told her where he was living. He
could be on the mainland for all she knew. Over two
thousand miles away, and as remote as he had ever been.

She supposed she ought to go downstairs and find the
coffee shop. Maybe, with something to eat and several
cups of coffee inside her she would feel more capable
of handling the situation. Right now, she had the horrible
suspicion that her journey had been a waste of time, and
she couldn't help remembering that Pierce had threat-
ened to fire her if she didn't return within the week.

Stepping out on to the verandah, she rested her hands
on the iron rail and looked down at the street below.
There were few people walking, but there were plenty
of cars using the connection between Kalakaua Avenue
and Kapiolani Boulevard; long expensive limousines,
driven by the more affluent members of the community,
through to topless beach buggies, rattling along at a
reckless pace.

But Laura hardly saw them. She was thinking about
Pierce and his objections to her trip. Of course, he had
not known before she left exactly what she would find
in San Francisco, any more than she had. Even so, when
she had 'phoned him from Pamela's apartment after her

sister had been taken to the hospital, he had not shown a lot of sympathy. Pierce Carver was used to getting his own way, and that did not include losing his secretary at a significant point in his latest book.

Laura sighed. As the author of some fifteen novels, and popularly regarded as the doyen of psychological thrillers, Pierce would survive, whatever happened. Pamela might not. For the next few days, he would have to persevere with the dictaphone he had acquired some years ago, and if that was not satisfactory, he would no doubt make other arrangements. Whether those 'arrangements' would involve her dismissal, Laura could not be absolutely sure. Pierce was artistic and temperamental, and he tended to say things in anger he did not actually mean. Not that she considered herself indispensable, of course. No one was that. But she had worked for him for almost three years, and she knew his idiosyncrasies so well.

She remembered his dismay when she had told him about Pamela's 'phone call. 'But you can't just walk out on me, Laura,' he had wailed. 'We're at the most crucial stage of the book. Whatever slough of despond your sister has got herself into cannot—*simply cannot*—be allowed to interfere with your obligations to me. Heavens, the girl's not a child, is she? She's over twenty-one. You're her sister, not her mother!'

There had been more of the same, but Laura had had no time to listen. She had been too busy making 'phone calls of her own, to the airport, to the mini cab service, and packing her belongings, to give him her undivided attention. She was sorry she had to leave him in the lurch. She knew how he depended upon her. But Pamela depended on her, too, and the apprehension she felt about her sister over-ruled her remorse.

She was so relieved they had been in England when the call came through. For the past four weeks, she had been staying in Aix, at the villa in Provence, which Pierce had rented to write his latest novel. Had he not grown bored with his surroundings, had he not felt the need for a change of scenery, he would not have suggested flying back to London, and there was no doubt now he regretted his decision to return home.

'You know how much I enjoy *our* sessions,' he had protested, when the issue of the dictaphone had been raised. 'Without your reactions, how will I know if I'm on the right track?'

'You managed perfectly well before I came on the scene,' Laura had pointed out swiftly, but in so doing, she had given Pierce the opening he was looking for.

'So I did,' he had remarked acidly, folding his arms as he was prone to do in moments of stress. 'So I did. Beware I don't decide I can manage without you. There are plenty of out-of-work secretaries simply panting to take your place!'

He was right. Laura knew that; and it had been with a certain amount of trepidation that she had told him she was taking a week's leave of absence with or without his consent. Pierce could be vindictive at times, and he might just decide to be awkward. She could only hope he would find it less easy to choose a replacement than he imagined, and that absence would achieve what reasoned argument could not.

With a feeling of anxious frustration, Laura abandoned this particular line of thought, and walked back into the bedroom. The hospital, she thought suddenly. She ought to ring the hospital and find out how Pamela was progressing. It had been eight o'clock, San Francisco time, when she last made an inquiry, and despite the doctor's assurance that her sister would pull through, her mental state was so precarious, Laura couldn't quite believe them.

The night staff at Mount Rushmore were reassuring. Pamela had had a reasonably good day and she was sleeping. The toxic level of her blood was falling, and if her psychological report proved satisfactory, she might be allowed to go home in a couple of days.

'There's no physical danger then?' Laura persisted, remembering articles she had read about toxic hepatitis and stomach bleeding.

'It seems unlikely,' replied the charge nurse smoothly. 'I think your sister's mental state is what we need to monitor. You do realise, don't you, she could always try this again?'

She realised, Laura reflected tensely, replacing the receiver. That was why she was here, in Honolulu. That was why she had agreed to contact Jason, on her sister's behalf. Naturally, she hadn't told Pamela of his relationship to Mike Kazantis, but after her sister confessed that Mike was no longer using the address he had put on his letters, there had seemed no alternative but to ask Jason's assistance. She had reassured Pamela with the conviction that if Jason could help, he would, but she had not really believed it. Still, she was prepared to do anything to take that look of desperation from her sister's face, and if it meant humbling herself before Jason Montefiore—and his brother-in-law—she would do it.

Unable to stand the inactivity any longer, Laura gathered up her bag and left the room. It was obvious Jason was unlikely to call this evening. Even if he got her message, which was by no means a foregone conclusion, he would evidently be in no hurry to contact her. If Phil Logan's attitude was anything to go by, he might not even acknowledge her call, and the prospect of having to tell Pamela she had failed was not something she wanted to contemplate.

The coffee shop was crowded and deciding she couldn't stand to wait, Laura left the hotel and headed towards the floodlit brilliance of Kalakaua Avenue. After the comparative quiet of her room, Waikiki's main thoroughfare was decidedly noisy, but she welcomed the activity to numb her anxious brain.

Finding a fast-food establishment, she ordered a burger and some coffee, and then carried her tray to a plastic booth and tried to swallow the sandwich. It wasn't easy. She realised belatedly a bowl of soup or some salad might have gone down more smoothly, but it was too late now to have second thoughts. Picking sesame seeds from the roll, she wondered if Phil Logan would tell her how she might get in touch with Mike Kazantis if Jason's whereabouts were *verboten*. Or had he orders to avoid *any* awkward inquiries? It was always possible that Jason had known of Mike's involvement with her sister, and obviously he would not want *his* sister to be upset. Laura cupped her chin on one hand. Whatever happened, it was unlikely that either Mike or his wife lived in the islands. Mike worked for Jason's father, and so far as she knew, Marco Montefiore's interests did not encroach on his son's territory.

Laura's lips twisted. How on earth had Pamela got herself involved with the Montefiore family? The brief conversation she had had with her sister had not elicited that kind of information. Besides, so far as she knew, Pamela did not know of Mike's connection with the Montefiores, and it was possible, that as Mrs Goldstein's private therapist, they could have met socially. Even if her sister had known the truth behind Laura's own break-up with Jason, she could still have become infatuated with Kazantis. There was nothing to connect him with Laura's abortive liaison, and if Kazantis had known of the association, he was unlikely to mention it to Pamela, for obvious reasons.

Pushing the burger aside, Laura lifted the plastic beaker containing her coffee and thoughtfully sipped the fragrant brew. American coffee was always so good, she mused inconsequently. Even the unimaginative container could not spoil the taste of its contents.

Gazing blindly out through the open doors on to the busy street beyond, she wondered again what she would do if her efforts to reach either Jason or his brother-in-law proved useless. And why—even if by some chance she did get to speak to Jason—did she think he might be able, or willing, to help her? What did she really expect him to do? What *could* he do? Mike Kazantis was his sister's *husband*. Surely, it was the height of arrogance to believe he might put Pamela's well-being before that of Irene.

It seemed an insoluble problem, and her brain ached with the effort of trying to solve it. She was not at all convinced that approaching Mike Kazantis was the right thing to do. If Pamela had been more reasonable, if she had been prepared to go back to England, as soon as she was fit, Laura was sure they would have found a way to sort things out. One parent families were not so unusual these days, if Pamela wanted to keep her baby. And if not, there were always adoption agencies eager and willing to find the child a good home.

But Pamela had not been reasonable. Her unwilling return to consciousness to find her sister at her bedside and, it transpired, in possession of all the facts of her case, had elicited an entirely different response. 'There

must be some mistake,' she had insisted, the faith she
had lost so drastically returning now that Laura was
there to listen. 'Mike wouldn't just abandon me. He
wouldn't! Something must be wrong. Perhaps he's been
taken ill, or had an accident. If only there was someone
we could ask. Someone who could give us a clue to his
whereabouts. Is there no one you know, Laura? No one
you met while you were over here?'

Whether Pamela knew exactly what she was asking,
Laura had no idea. Certainly she had never confided the
true facts of her relationship with Jason Montefiore to
her sister. But perhaps Pamela sensed, or suspected, that
there had been more to Laura's abrupt return to England
than the casual explanation that she had grown tired of
living so far from London. Whatever, Laura had felt
compelled to use what influence she had to try and set
her sister's mind at rest, and that was why she was here
in Hawaii, facing the increasing conviction that she was
wasting her time.

The situation seemed hardly brighter in the morning.
Laura had not slept well, and after ringing the hospital
and ensuring herself that Pamela was still making pro-
gress, she considered what her next move should be. She
could ring the club again, she supposed, although
the prospect was not one she favoured. Besides, only the
cleaning staff were likely to be there at this hour of
the morning, and none of them would risk their jobs by
giving out private information. And perhaps she was being overly pessimistic anyway. Jason might telephone.
There was still time.

The telephone rang while she was in the shower, but
although she dashed out of the bathroom to take the call,
a towel wrapped hastily around her dripping body, it was

an early morning call meant for someone else. '*Aloha*, this is your wake-up service,' announced the mechanical voice, and Laura slammed down the receiver, feeling the painful ache of tears behind her eyes.

Dressed again, in the cotton pants and shirt she had worn the evening before, she stood in front of the mirror to plait her hair. She had no particular desire to look at her reflection, the evidence of the disturbed nights she had spent since Pamela's call a visual depressant. But she couldn't help assessing her appearance with Jason's critical eyes, and her conclusion was not flattering. Too tall, too thin, and too plain, she thought bitterly, wondering, not for the first time, whatever it was he had seen in her. She was certainly nothing like the girls who had worked in his club or hung around the bar, hoping to attract his attention. They had all had one thing in common: an unswerving faith in their own desirability, whereas Laura had always doubted her appeal.

She sighed now, her hands falling limply to her sides. From the very beginning, she had been bemused by Jason's interest in her, and perhaps that was why he had succeeded where other men had failed. If she had not been so naïvely flattered by his attentions, she might have recognised him sooner for what he was, instead of learning too late how easily she had been deceived.

She shook her head. It was too late now to change the past. And in spite of her experiences, she had succeeded in making a new life for herself with Pierce. There had actually been days when she had not thought about Jason Montefiore and the devastating influence he had had on her. Until Pamela's 'phone call, that was, and the inescapable connotations it had aroused...

It was barely eight o'clock when she went down to the coffee shop and ordered some coffee. The menu didn't interest her, but realising that starving herself would help no one, she chose scrambled eggs and toast. Trying to do them justice, she surveyed her fellow diners enviously. How nice it would have been to have nothing more momentous on her mind than what bikini she would wear to the beach, Laura mused wryly. With her pale skin, she was definitely a rarity, and it was not a distinction she enjoyed.

After the waitress had taken away her half-eaten plate of eggs, Laura sipped her third cup of coffee and wondered what she ought to do now. She supposed she should stay around the hotel, if only to be on hand should Jason make an attempt to contact her. On the other hand, if he had not 'phoned by lunchtime, she could surely discount his doing so, and then she would have to decide whether or not to try the club in person.

Her decision made, she told the receptionist at the desk she was expecting a call, and then joined the other holidaymakers congregating beside the small pool. Seated in the shade on a padded lounger, she made an effort to appear as nonchalant as the other guests, but she was acutely alert to the paging call of the receptionist's voice.

From time to time, a lissom Polynesian girl, dressed in a flowered bikini, with a matching kanga looped about her waist, came to offer cocktails, fruit drinks or coffee. But Laura always refused her lilting inquiry, and when a shadow fell across her for the fourth time, she lifted her head impatiently.

'Thank you, I don't want...' she was beginning rather tersely, when her throat dried and the words choked to silence in her mouth. 'Heavens—*Jason*!' she got out disbelievingly, scrambling hastily to her feet, but her knees felt ridiculously unsteady as she faced the man across the width of the lounger.

CHAPTER TWO

'HELLO, LAURA.'

Jason's voice was cool and polite, his tone detached and incurious, as if her arrival in the islands was no surprise to him. On the contrary, there was a cynical gleam in the depths of his pale gold eyes, and his expression was resigned and only slightly guarded.

'I...er...I thought you'd ring,' Laura stammered now, caught unaware by her own unwelcome response to his dark magnetism. She had thought she had recovered from that unhealthy infatuation, but it seemed she had been premature in dismissing his attraction.

'I did,' he replied briefly, shifting his weight from one foot to the other, and she noticed, inconsequently, how much older he looked. The lines that etched his dark features were deeply ingrained, and the hair that lay so smoothly against his head was distinctly threaded with grey. 'You were not available,' he added, glancing behind him to where two other men were lounging by the pool bar.

Realising he had not come alone, Laura felt a resurgence of the resentment which had sustained her through the long weeks following her return to England. Of course, she thought bitterly, a man like him would need a bodyguard. He must have many enemies, not just here, but on the mainland.

'I rang yesterday evening,' he continued, observing her changing expression with impassive eyes. 'Logan said it was urgent. I presume he exaggerated.'

'I…why…*no*!' Laura gathered her wandering thoughts, and adopted an air of concentration. 'He— Logan, that is—doubted you would wish to speak to me. I'm afraid I went for a walk. You should have left a message.'

Jason expelled his breath evenly. 'Yes,' he said flatly. 'Yes, I expect I should. Well—I am here now. I suggest we find somewhere we can talk.'

'Oh—yes.' Laura looked about her awkwardly, realising for the first time that their conversation was being observed by at least a dozen pairs of curious eyes. And why not, she reflected drily. They must be wondering what a man like Jason Montefiore could possibly want with a pale-skinned English girl of nondescript appearance, when he could evidently have his pick of any of the golden-skinned beauties lining the pool.

'I assume you have no objections to coming with me?' Jason inquired, as they walked towards the hotel entrance, and Laura cast him a sideways glance.

'Coming with you?' she echoed faintly, acutely aware of the shortcomings of her outfit compared to the fine silk of his beige suit.

'I thought we might use the yacht,' he essayed politely, allowing her to precede him into the hotel. 'We can hardly talk here.'

'Why not?'

Laura's braid swung over one shoulder as she twisted her head towards him, and his lips parted in a thin smile. 'I think we will use the yacht,' he responded, striding lithely through the lobby and pushing wide the swing door for her to precede him out on to the front steps of the building. 'You initiated this meeting, Laura,' he added crisply. 'The least you can do is to allow me to choose its venue.'

Aware of the two men from the bar following them, Laura had little choice but to step out into the sunlight. Rubbing her palms against her upper arms, she saw the sleek silver Mercedes waiting at the kerb, and her heart beat a little faster in spite of her misgivings.

Jason went ahead of her down the steps, and she saw him loosen the button beneath his tie and pull the knot away from his collar. So even he felt the heat, she reflected tensely, glad of the small imperfection. Then, as the doors opened behind her, she descended the steps, just as a uniformed chauffeur emerged to open the car doors for them.

'Get in,' advised Jason briefly, his eyes already looking beyond her to the two men behind. She did so, with reluctance, closing her ears to the terse instructions Jason was issuing, not looking his way again even when she felt the depression of his weight on the cushioned seat beside her.

The door was closed, and immediately the air-conditioning inside the car chilled her flesh. With the glass screen between front and back raised, they were enclosed in a world of smoked glass sophistication, and Laura couldn't help remembering the last occasion she had ridden with him. There had been antagonism between them then, as there was now, but also a compelling familiarity—an addictive intimacy Laura had found it so hard to live without. She had known him so well— or at least she had thought she had—and there were times in those early days when she had wondered how she had ever found the strength to leave him, even after what she had learned. The truth, she had discovered to her cost, was that love did not always conform to a code of ethics. It was headstrong and unpredictable, and it had taken many months and many sleepless nights to get Jason Montefiore out of her blood...

'You flew in—when? Yesterday?' he inquired now, and she was forced to withdraw her attention from the leather strap hanging by the window.

'Yesterday afternoon,' she agreed, giving him a swift look of appraisal. He had lost weight, she noticed unwillingly, but the deeply-set eyes and thin-lipped mouth were still as disturbingly sensual as ever. His cheeks had hollowed, but the skin stretched tautly over his bones gave his dark face the strength and character she remembered, his Italian ancestry only evident in the burnished darkness of his hair.

'From London?' he persisted, raising one leg to rest his ankle across his knee, and the fine cloth of his pants tautened across his thighs.

'No,' she responded shortly, turning her eyes away from his unconscious sexuality, and concentrating on the back of the chauffeur's head. Evidently the two other men were riding in a separate car, for there was only themselves and the driver in this one. After all, what use had Jason for a bodyguard with her? He was perfectly capable of subduing her, should he so wish.

She thought he might pursue his questions, but he didn't. As if deciding he could wait if she could, he lounged a little lower in his seat, resting one leanfingered hand on his drawn-up ankle and gazing broodingly out of the tinted window.

It didn't take them long to reach the marina. Jason's driver evidently knew the city well, and in only a few minutes they had reached the basin where dozens of yachts had their mooring. The Mercedes drove into the parking area, but before he could get out to open the door for his passengers, Jason had already taken care of it.

'You can pick me up at four o'clock,' he told the man, flicking back the cuff of his brown silk shirt and glancing at the narrow gold watch circling his wrist. 'If I need you before, I'll call.'

'Yes, sir.'

The chauffeur touched his cap with exaggerated courtesy, and Jason's lean face displayed the first trace of humour Laura had seen since his appearance. 'Okay, Ben,' he acknowledged drily, jerking open Laura's door and offering her his hand to alight. 'I'll see you later.'

Laura got out without any assistance, and Jason's hand fell to his side without comment. Slamming the door behind her, he waited until his driver had moved away before starting off towards the boardwalk, his long stride covering the ground easily so that Laura had to hurry to keep up.

He was one of the few men who did not make her conscious of her height, she thought reluctantly, his lean frame overtaking hers by a good six inches. It was one of the first things she had noticed about him; that, and the lazy brilliance of his eyes. The fact that he had been at least ten years older than she was had not registered. Despite the fact that until then she had never been interested in older men, her attraction to Jason had been immediate and overwhelming. Was that how it had been with Pamela? she wondered, struggling manfully to remember exactly why she was here.

Jason's yacht, the *Laura M*, was moored at the end of the jetty. Laura had thought he might have changed the yacht—or changed its name—but the 84 foot schooner was exactly as she remembered it, its trim white lines gleaming as it nudged against the boardwalk. A man in white shorts and a knitted cotton shirt was already on board, leaning on the rail, talking to a member of the crew of the adjoining craft. But he quickly straightened when he saw Jason, and Laura's lips parted as she recognised Alec Cowray, the captain of the *Laura M.*

'Good morning, Mr Montefiore,' he greeted Jason politely, lifting his cap and then pushing it back on his bald pate. 'I didna expect ye to be coming aboard this day.'

'I didn't know myself, Mr Cowray,' responded Jason drily, stepping on to the deck. 'Don't disturb yourself. I shan't be staying longer than a few hours. I gather we do have some food on board?'

'No problem,' averred the stout Scotsman, his expression mirroring his confusion, and then he saw Laura. '*Christ!*' he exclaimed, forgetting to moderate his language. 'I don't believe it!'

'Hello, Mr Cowray. How are you?' asked Laura awkwardly, following Jason towards the forward hatch. 'It's good to see you again.'

'It's good to see you, too, miss,' declared Alec Cowray fervently. He looked helplessly towards his employer. 'Will that be lunch for two, Mr Montefiore?'

'Provisionally,' replied Jason crisply, giving Laura a thoughtful glance. 'Don't go to a lot of trouble, Alec. Miss Huyton may not be staying.'

Laura pressed her lips together to prevent herself from voicing an indignant comment as she followed Jason down the gleaming stairway. She was more convinced than ever now that he knew exactly why she had come to the islands, and she fed her resentment in an effort to dispel the effect her surroundings were having on her. He had brought her here deliberately, she thought, knowing what association it would have for her. The first time

Jason had made love with her had been aboard this yacht, and she averted her eyes determinedly from the panelled doors to his stateroom. She knew the craft so well—she knew there were three suites; an upper and lower saloon; and a well-equipped galley aft. Yet, for all its size, a crew of three could handle it, using the powerful diesel engines when the sails were not in use.

Jason led the way into the forward saloon, a beautifully furnished living area, with cushioned banquettes, panelled walls, and a soft carpet underfoot. From its windows on three sides, one had an uninterrupted view when the craft was sailing, and Laura remembered moonlit evenings, after she and Jason had dined alone, sitting here and enjoying the starlit beauty of the night...

'Will you have a drink?'

While she had been absorbing the saloon's familiarity, Jason had opened up the fitted bar and was presently examining its contents. 'Gin? Scotch? Vodka? Or would you like me to mix you a Chi-Chi?' he inquired, mentioning the island cocktail which had once been her favourite.

'Nothing, thank you,' she responded tautly, seating herself on the low banquette and imprisoning her hands between her knees. 'I—well, I'd like to get this over with. I believe you know why I've come.'

Jason poured himself a scotch, despite the early hour, and after adding several cubes of ice, looked at her over the rim of the glass. 'I have a fairly good idea,' he conceded cynically, swallowing a generous mouthful. 'I suppose you assume my agreeing to see you gives you the edge. Well—I shouldn't bank on it, if I were you.'

Laura felt the colour pour into her cheeks at his scathing words, and it was all she could do to remain sitting.

But standing would be equally as perilous, and she didn't want him to see how nervous she really was.

'I have no—preconceptions,' she declared now, holding up her head and concentrating on the tasselled cord securing a fall of velvet curtain. The words stuck in her throat, but she had to say them: 'I'm—grateful—you agreed to see me.'

Jason lowered his glass. 'Did you think I wouldn't?' he inquired mockingly, and she bent her head to study the tightly clenched bones of her knees.

'I thought it was possible,' she agreed carefully. 'As I said before, Logan didn't seem to think...'

'Phil Logan was only doing his job as he saw it. He knows we split up. I guess he got the wrong idea.'

Laura quivered, and when she lifted her eyes to his, the resentment she was feeling was mirrored in their depths. 'You mean—he thought you got tired of me, don't you?' she demanded painfully. 'Did you disabuse him?'

'You're here, aren't you?' remarked Jason flatly. 'That should mean something, even to Logan.'

Laura absorbed his words with a troubled frown. 'You're—very generous,' she murmured unwillingly. 'I—don't know what to say.'

'I'm sure you'll think of something,' retorted Jason tersely, finishing the scotch in his glass. 'I suggest you tell me what you've been doing since you left. I know; but I'd like to hear it in your words, just so we understand one another.'

Laura caught her breath. 'What do you mean?' she exclaimed, shaking her head. 'You—*know*—what I've been doing?'

Jason sighed. 'Must we go into this right now?'

'Yes, I think we must.'

'Okay.' He set down his glass, and came to stand in front of her. 'But first, I think I should sample the merchandise, don't you? I mean, it has been three years, and I may have overestimated your appeal!' And before she could move or even comprehend his meaning, he had circled her wrist with his fingers and jerked her to her feet.

The warm strength of his lean fingers on her nape, as he drew her unresistingly towards him, was the last coherent awareness Laura had before his lips descended on hers. Disbelief; resentment; *panic*; all were briefly subdued by the hard pressure of his mouth, and her shaken disconcertment opened her lips to his tongue.

His free arm slid around her, drawing her closer into his embrace, and it was the sensuous abrasion of his shirt against her fingers that brought her a returning measure of sanity. But although she fought free of him without too much effort, his shocking behaviour had disturbed her, and she knew he had sensed her involuntary response.

'How—how dare you?' she got out, when her breathing had steadied, and she saw the wary gleam that entered his eyes at her words.

'How dare I?' he asked, echoing her question. 'What did you expect? An apology?' He shook his head. 'I'm sorry. I don't feel I have anything to apologise for.'

Laura blinked. 'What are you talking about?'

Jason expelled his breath heavily. 'Laura, let's stop playing these games, shall we? You know why you're here, and I know why you're here. Okay—maybe I did precipitate matters a little, but you can't deny you wanted it, just as much as I did.'

Laura gulped. 'There's some mistake...'

'Is there?'

'Yes.' Her tongue circled her lips with increasing rapidity. 'I...I don't know what—kind of an advantage you think Pamela's situation gives you, but—but so far as I am concerned...'

'Wait a minute!' Jason's harsh voice broke into her stammered outburst, and she broke off at once, staring at him with troubled eyes. 'Run that by me again,' he said grimly. '*Who* is Pamela?'

'You know who Pamela is,' she exclaimed. 'Pamela Huyton. My *sister* Pamela. Don't pretend you don't know about her and Mike!'

Jason fell back a step, still regarding her with distinct incredulity. 'Your sister Pamela?' he repeated blankly. 'What the hell would I know about your sister, for Christ's sake? And Mike? Mike who?'

'Mike Kazantis!' declared Laura quickly, trembling a little as she struggled to take the initiative. 'You know who Mike Kazantis is, don't you? Or are you going to deny all knowledge of his identity, too?'

Jason's mouth thinned. 'Are you trying to tell me that your sister is in some way involved with Mike Kazantis?' he inquired tautly, and Laura nodded.

'But you know,' she said bitterly. 'You know you do. Else why did you agree to see me? Unless you thought you could gloat over our misfortunes!'

Jason's dark features lost all expression, and the lines that bracketed his nose and mouth looked that much more pronounced. 'Is that the opinion you have of me?' he said sombrely. 'Well, well! You really thought I would do a thing like that?'

Laura was not a little confused by now, and in spite of her determination not to let him get the better of her, his quiet words had more than an element of truth in them. But why—if he hadn't known about his brother-in-law—why had he said he knew why she was here?

'Wheth—whether you knew or not, you do now,' she said, forcing herself to go on. 'Pamela is in the hospital in San Francisco. She took an overdose of sleeping tablets. She'll live, but I don't know for how long.'

Jason's nostrils flared, and with a curious inclination of his head, he moved away towards the bar. Then, swinging round, he poured himself a second glass of scotch, tipping his head back to drink it before turning again to face her.

'It...it's barely eleven o'clock,' Laura exclaimed abruptly, unable to prevent the words from spilling from her lips. 'Is it wise to—to drink so much?'

Jason's lips twisted. 'Not wise at all,' he conceded sardonically. 'But that's my problem, not yours. So. Go on about your sister. Why don't you think she'll survive?'

'Because she's pregnant!' Laura pressed the palms of her hands together. 'And Kazantis has deserted her.'

'Deserted her?' Jason considered the phrase. 'What an old-fashioned expression! You mean, I suppose, that as soon as he discovered your sister had a problem, he took off.'

Laura blinked. 'He doesn't know about the baby.' She frowned. 'At least, I think he doesn't.' It was something she had not thought to ask her sister.

'I'd guess he does,' retorted Jason drily. 'If indeed it is Mike's.'

'What do you mean?' Laura was indignant. 'Pamela wouldn't lie about something like that!'

'And she says it's his?'

'Yes.' Laura drew a trembling breath. 'Do you know where he is?'

'Kazantis? Right now?' Jason shrugged. 'I'd say—Europe.'

'Europe!' Laura blanched. 'Where in Europe?'

'Italy.' Jason dropped his empty glass back on to the bar. 'At least that's where Irene is, so...'

'Italy!' Laura's shoulders sagged. 'Oh, God! Why did he have to be there?'

'I'm not saying I know it for a fact,' said Jason evenly. 'But, like I said, Irene is there right now, visiting my grandparents. And, knowing my father's ideas about his women, I'd say he'd insist she didn't go unescorted.'

Laura sank down weakly on to the banquette behind her. 'For how long?' she asked helplessly. 'When will they be coming back?'

'One month, maybe two. Who knows?' Jason lifted his shoulders in a dismissing gesture. 'I'm not my sister's keeper.'

Laura shook her head, resting her elbows on her knees and cupping her cheeks in her hot palms. 'Oh, God!' she said again, feeling the emptiness of despair gripping her insides. 'What am I going to do?'

It was only partly a rhetorical question, but the sudden breeze through the open door alerted her to the fact that Jason had left her. She was alone in the green and gold beauty of the saloon, alone with her unwilling memories, and with the terrifying realisation that there was nothing she could do.

She supposed she should leave. After all, Jason had done what he could. He had told her where Kazantis was, and he had not disbelieved her story. The anger he might have displayed at the news that Pamela had evidently been having an affair with his sister's husband had not materialised, and she was simply wasting her time, and his, by pursuing the matter further. Somehow,

she was going to have to find a way to tell Pamela that
Mike Kazantis was married; that there was no point in
her threatening to kill herself again, because he could
not marry her. Not unless he got a divorce from Irene,
of course, and if Jason was right and he was with his
wife, in Italy, that did not seem at all likely. Besides
which, Laura had met Irene, and she knew her to be a
very beautiful young woman. It had been an outside
chance at best that her marriage to Kazantis had floun-
dered. Remembering what she knew of him, Laura
doubted anything would prise him away from the wealth
and influence that came from being Marco Montefiore's
son-in-law, and contacting Jason had been her last resort.

Which brought her back to that other puzzling development: why had Jason assumed he knew why she was
in Hawaii? Was there something she had overlooked?
Did he know something she didn't know? And why had
he kissed her? She had been prepared to face his anger,
not his passion.

With trembling fingers, she traced the bare contours
of her lips. She wore little in the way of cosmetics, just
eyeliner and mascara, and occasionally a shiny lip-gloss
to frame her mouth. But what little make-up she had
been wearing had been erased by his caress, and she
couldn't deny the unwilling awareness that his touch still
had the power to melt her bones. If only...

His reappearance with an enamelled beaker which he
held out to her arrested her guilty thoughts. 'Here,' he
said, pushing it into her hand. 'You look as though you
could use it.'

'What is it?' she asked foolishly, while the aromatic
odour of ground beans floated to her nostrils, and Jason's
mouth pulled down.

'Just coffee,' he replied drily, taking off his jacket and

pulling off his tie. 'Laced with heroin, of course!' He grimaced. 'Drink it, for God's sake! I'm not reduced to drugging my women yet!'

Laura obediently sipped the fragrant beverage, recovering a little of her composure in the time it took her to drink it. Jason, she noticed, tossed his jacket and tie aside and flung himself on to the wide velvet cushions at the broad forward end of the cabin, crossing his legs as he had done before and staring broodingly out on to the sunlit dock.

'So, tell me what happened,' he said at length, when he had given her time to compose herself. 'How did your sister meet Kazantis?'

'I don't know.' Laura caught her lower lip between her teeth before continuing: 'She works—*worked*—in Sausalito, but she has an apartment in San Francisco.'

'Since when?'

'Oh eighteen months, I suppose. She qualified as a physiotherapist in London, but she wanted to travel. I tried to dissuade her from coming to the United States, but...'

'...she wouldn't listen?'

'Right.' Laura looked down into her cup. 'She always seemed so much younger than me. It's only two years, I know, but—well, I've always felt much older.'

'And you didn't want her to venture out into the bold bad world!' remarked Jason wryly, running his hand inside the opened neckline of his shirt and in so doing loosening several more buttons. 'So—she met Kazantis. Why didn't you warn her?'

'Warn her?' Laura looked across the cabin at him, uncomfortably aware of the sensuality of his exploring hand. The skin of his chest exposed by his careless movements was as brown and smooth as she remembered, his nipples taut, an arrowing of fine hair only lightly roughening his flesh. 'I didn't know.'

'She didn't write to you?'

'Well, yes. Yes, of course, she wrote.' Laura dragged her eyes away, and tried to keep her mind on what she was saying. 'She just didn't mention her relationship with Mike Kazantis, that's all. And...and after all, she wouldn't know who he was.'

'Who he was?'

'Yes.' Laura shifted a little restlessly. 'Your brother-in-law; Irene's husband! I...she...we never discussed your relations.'

Jason regarded her intently. 'But she knew of me? She knew we were living together, didn't she?'

Laura moistened her lips. 'She knew we were...close, yes.'

'But did she know we were living together?' persisted Jason insistently, and Laura wondered if he already knew the answer.

'It's not important,' she said, shaking her head, but he did not agree.

'Perhaps, if you'd been more honest with her, she would have felt more able to confide in you,' he commented brusquely, and Laura met his relentless gaze with hastily-summoned indignation.

'Are you saying it's my fault?' she exclaimed, using anger as a means to avoid his questioning, and he shrugged.

'I'm saying you were afraid to tell your sister the truth. Why should you be surprised if she feels like-wise?'

Laura sniffed, and buried her nose in the beaker. 'That's a simplistic way of looking at things,' she said, in a muffled voice.

'I'm a simplistic person,' he responded carelessly, and she thought how ironic it was that he should say a thing like that.

'You're the least simplistic person I know,' she retorted childishly. 'Oh, for heaven's sake, does it matter what I did or didn't tell her? Pamela's pregnant, right? And if I hadn't arrived when I did, she would have been dead!'

Jason considered her for a few nerve-racking moments, then he said quietly: 'Exactly why did you arrive in California?'

'Pamela 'phoned me.' Laura cradled the beaker between her palms and gazed into space. 'I'd just got back from Aix...'

'The South of France, I know.'

'...and when she rang...' Laura paused briefly, as the import of what he had said reminded her of something he had said earlier— 'when she rang, I sensed something was wrong.'

'Just sensed?'

'No. No.' Laura spread a helpless hand. 'Pamela sounded strange—desperate! I don't know why, but I knew she had to have rung for a purpose.'

'A cry for help?' suggested Jason drily, and Laura looked at him sharply.

'Don't you believe me?'

'Oh, yes.' He tilted his head back against the dark green velvet and studied her through narrowed eyes. 'But, objectively, I'd say that perhaps your sister wasn't as desperate to kill herself as you might think. I mean, she did rig herself a lifeline before jumping over the side, metaphorically speaking, of course.'

Laura sat up straighter. 'That's a rotten thing to suggest!'

'It's something for you to think about,' retorted Jason flatly. 'Laura, I hear of people over-dosing every day. Most of them do a better job of it than your sister appears to have done.'

'You…you swine!'

Laura set down the cup and got unsteadily to her feet, but before she could make it to the door, Jason was there before her. 'The simplistic view, remember?' he said, his back against the panels successfully blocking her exit. 'Laura, I'm not saying Pamela did this to gain attention, but it has been known. Remember that.'

'Will you get out of my way?'

Laura's hands clenched at her sides as she waited for him to move, but he didn't. 'Eventually,' he averred, his tawny eyes resolute between the dark fringe of his lashes. 'Go sit down. We haven't finished our conversation.'

'I have.'

'Do you want me to use force?' he inquired lazily, his eyes moving down over her high small breasts thrusting against the thin material of her shirt, to the slender curve of her hips outlined by the tie-waisted cotton pants, and she immediately abandoned her mission.

'I don't know what else we can possibly have to say to one another,' she exclaimed, moving back into the middle of the floor and wrapping her arms about herself, as if for protection. 'You've made your position very clear. Why won't you let me go?'

Jason straightened away from the door, but he didn't shift his stance. 'What are you going to do?' he asked. 'Now that your attempt to find your sister's lover and speak with him has failed, what are you going to tell Pamela?'

'I don't know.' Laura shook her head a trifle wearily.

'I'll think of something. If I can persuade her to come back to London with me...'

'And if you can't?'

'Oh, please!' Laura turned away from him, gazing out through the window, across the blue waters of the yacht basin. 'Why should you care? Our lives mean nothing to you!'

'Yours does,' he retorted crisply, and she turned her head and gazed at him over her shoulder as if she couldn't believe her ears.

'What did you say?'

'You heard me,' he responded tersely, folding his arms across his chest. 'Why else do you suppose I've had your movements monitored, ever since you ran out on me? I know all about your life in London, and that creep, Pierce Carver, you've been living with for the past two and a half years.'

Laura half turned, her lips parting incredulously. 'I— I am not *living* with Pierce,' she protested, indignation vying with disbelief. 'I work with him, yes, but that's all. Your investigator was wrong if he told you there was anything between us.'

'You live at his house!'

'I have a room there. I also have a flat of my own,' retorted Laura hotly, and then anger quickly enveloped her. 'But that's my business. I don't have to explain myself to you! It's nothing to do with you! I said it before and I'll say it again: how dare you?'

Jason regarded her beneath lowered brows. 'Why didn't he come with you to San Francisco?' he demanded harshly. 'Doesn't he care about your sister?'

'Why should he?' Laura was trembling with resentment. 'Oh! I can't believe this, I really can't! You've actually been having me followed ever since I left Hawaii?'

Jason shrugged, making no immediate response. Then he said flatly, 'I want you back, Laura. But you should know that. I didn't want you to leave. That was why I thought you'd come back to Hawaii. I—foolishly, I now realise—imagined you had had second thoughts; that the feelings you used to say you had for me had overwhelmed your much vaunted scruples. I was wrong. I admit it. But that doesn't alter the situation. I still want you—for the present, at least. Seeing you again has only confirmed that belief. And I'm prepared to go to practically any lengths to get you—even if it means involving your sister!'

CHAPTER THREE

LAURA FELT as if someone had just delivered a gasping blow to her midriff. Her throat felt tight, and her breathing was suspended, the stunning reality of what Jason had said resounding in her head like the clanging of a bell.

'You're—not—serious!'

'But, I am.' Jason's expression was faintly self-derisive now. 'How could you doubt it? No one—but no one—walks out on Jason Montifore!'

'So that's it!' Laura caught her breath. 'Your pride was hurt!' she accused him bitterly, the shuddering intensity of his announcement tempered now by his mocking confession.

Jason inclined his head. 'If it pleases you to think so,' he remarked carelessly. 'I won't insult your intelligence by protesting I'm in love with you.'

'No. Don't.' Laura hunched her shoulders with sudden loathing. For a moment, for a brief space of time, she had half believed there must be some feeling behind his impassive pronouncement. But his taunting expression dispelled that assumption, and made a mockery of her sympathetic response.

'Nevertheless, I am prepared to do what I can to help you, providing you are equally prepared to do the same.'

Laura swallowed disbelievingly. 'Are you threatening me?'

'Threatening you? No. How could you think it?' he responded, in that same half mocking tone. 'I'm offering you a way out, an alternative your sister may find more appealing than a depressing plane ride back to London.'

Laura shifted uneasily. 'I don't understand you.'

'You will.' Jason shrugged. 'Stay and have lunch with me, and I'll explain.'

Laura moved her head from side to side, but it was a futile gesture. 'I don't see what you can say to appease Pamela's state of mind,' she insisted. 'She feels desperate and afraid…'

'Because she's alone and pregnant, and she has no future means of support,' said Jason levelly. 'Wouldn't you say that covered her immediate situation? That and her professed desire to see Kazantis again?'

'Well, yes…'

'Good.' Jason's arms fell to his sides and he gestured politely towards the cushioned seat behind her. 'So. Sit down. I'll go tell Alec we'll eat in fifteen minutes. You do like lobster, don't you?' His dark brows arched, and a faintly humorous gleam entered his eyes. 'Oh, yes, of course you do. How could I forget?'

As he pulled open the door behind him and went to inform the yacht's captain of his intentions, Laura curled one leg beneath her and sank down unhappily on to the soft banquette. It seemed he had all the answers, she thought bitterly, her fingers tugging convulsively at the fringe of braided silk that edged the cushions. And if he wasn't threatening her exactly, he was certainly using Pamela's condition to get what he wanted.

But why her? she brooded helplessly. Why was he prepared to go to such lengths to get her back? Was it only because she had walked out on him? Was he really so vain, that he couldn't bear the implications of her action? It was not an adjective she would have associated with him once, but how well had she really known him, after all? Once, she would have said she knew everything about him—his likes, his dislikes; his fairness, and his humour; the things that made him laugh, and the things that aroused his anger; his integrity in business, and his probity in justice. The men who worked for him and with him, respected him as well as liked him, and until experience had taught her differently, she had never had cause to doubt him.

Of course, she had been in love with him then, madly and irresistibly in love with a man she had never dreamed might be attracted to her. When she first went to work for him, as a temporary replacement for his own secretary, the other girls at the agency had teased her about his lean good looks, and the fact that he was one of the wealthiest men on the island. Naturally they, like her, had never imagined he would take any interest in a long-legged English girl, whose only claim to beauty was the silvery fair hair that fell almost to her waist. The rest of her features were totally ordinary, she knew: blue eyes, that watered when the sun was too strong, a straight nose that was not the least bit retroussé, and a wide mouth, whose lower lip was just the tiniest bit fuller. She discounted the length of her lashes, whose tips required mascara to be seen, and the slender curves of her figure. In her experience, men preferred smaller women, with fuller breasts, women who nestled into the curve of their arm instead of meeting them on eye-level terms.

Not that she had ever been able to say that of Jason. His height, and the lithe muscularity of his body, had always made her aware of her own femininity, and he had always maintained he preferred taller women. There had been plenty of them, goodness knows. Before she had figured in his scheme of things, he had had other mistresses, and there were several would-be supplicants all willing to inform Laura of how precarious her position was. Not to mention his ex-wife, Regina, and their daughter, Lucia...

She shook her head, banishing the unwilling memories of the emotions he had aroused. It was ridiculous, she told herself desperately. How could she even consider his demands? She couldn't stay in Hawaii. She couldn't abandon Pierce in the middle of the new book. Her life was in England now. Her job was in England. She had to make him understand she could not abdicate her responsibilities.

Three years ago, things had been different. Pamela had been training at a good teaching hospital in London, and sharing a flat with several other nurses. When Laura had been given the opportunity to spend six months in the Honolulu branch of the international secretarial agency in Bond Street, where she had worked at that time, it had seemed a marvellous break. It had been no wrench to give up her bedsitter, put the few belongings she was not taking with her into storage, and fly off to Hawaii. But not now. Now, she had her own flat, in Highgate. She had put down roots, and she was no longer the carefree twenty-two-year-old she had been when Jason first met her. Besides which, she didn't want to lose her job with Pierce. She liked working for him. The job was interesting, and it had given her a chance to travel, as well as providing a very generous salary. She couldn't give that up, not at the whim of a man who she despised. She should not have come here, she acknowledged belatedly. She should not have allowed Pamela's desperate plight to drive her into a situation she obviously could not handle. But then, she realised bleakly, she had had no way of knowing how Jason would react to her plea for help. She had never suspected he might have plans of his own.

'I've told Alec to have the awning erected.' Jason's lazy tones interrupted her reverie, and she turned her head to look at him. 'I thought we might eat on deck,' he continued. 'It's cool enough in the shade.'

Laura wanted to say she didn't want to eat lunch with him, but she bit back the words. There was no point in antagonising him, she decided weakly, ignoring the fact that the longer she allowed this charade to continue, the harder it would be to convince him she could not be blackmailed.

'All right,' she said now, indifferently, sliding her curled leg off the cushions and giving a little shrug. 'But I'm not very hungry.'

'Nor am I. My appetites run in an entirely different direction,' responded Jason unemotionally. 'But unless I miss my guess, you're not exactly in a mood to take advantage of them, are you?'

A wave of warm indignation swept over her skin at his careless words, and as if that was answer enough, Jason's lips twisted. 'I thought not,' he essayed, turning back to the bar. 'I suggest a cocktail instead. Something crisp, but not too sharp. I wouldn't want to sour what promises to be an…interesting association.'

Laura looked up at him tensely, and then, giving into a wholly ungovernable sense of panic, she sprang to her feet. 'I…I can't go through with this!' she exclaimed unsteadily. 'I don't care what you say, I won't let you blackmail me! If you can't help me find Mike Kazantis, I shall fly back to San Francisco tonight.'

Jason turned from pouring white rum into a metal mixer. 'Strong words,' he remarked, his expression wiped of all humour. 'However, much as I hate to say

this, you came to me, Laura. I didn't invite you here.
And as you have given me the means to keep you here,
why should I let you go?'

Laura swallowed. 'You can't force me to stay.'

'No. I can't do that,' he agreed, adding a measure of
orange curacao to the flask. 'Nor do I intend to do so. I
shall just make it—difficult for you to go.'

Laura gazed at him disbelievingly. 'How could you
do that?'

Jason shrugged, his attention fixed on the remaining
ingredients needed to complete the cocktail. 'Sit down,'
he advised evenly. 'Wait until you've heard what I have
to say. And stop looking so anxious.' His tawny eyes
lifted to her troubled face. 'The prospect of going to bed
with me used not to frighten you that much!'

Laura gulped and turned away. 'You're...despicable!'

'Why?' He fastened the cap on the container and
shook it energetically. 'Isn't it the truth? I seem to remember you were not exactly opposed to our making
love.'

'It was *not* love!'

'Would you know the difference?' he demanded cynically, and then he expelled his breath on a heavy sigh.
'Look. I don't want to argue with you, Laura. It's obvious we've got a lot of ground to make up. Right now,
I suggest you have a Mai Tai and stop worrying about
your fate. The future will take care of itself. It always
has, and it always will.'

The crushed ice frosting the glass he held out to her
was very appealing, and without really knowing why,
she accepted the cocktail. Perhaps she needed the support the alcohol could give her, she thought miserably,
sipping the chilled liquid. But it was delicious. She had

to admit that, if only to herself. Jason had lost none of his skill…in any direction, she added silently.

Out on deck, two white-coated stewards had just finished laying the table. Its glassy surface was spread with bamboo place mats and shining silver cutlery, pristine white napkins reflected in the polished gleam of delicate cut glass. From somewhere, a centrepiece of star jasmine and scarlet frangipani, called plumeria in the islands, had been arranged, and a bottle of Dom Perignon was residing in an ice bucket. Set beneath the striped awning, it was at once open to the soft trade winds, yet protected both from the sun, and the inquisitive glances of other users of the marina. A millionaire's retreat indeed, thought Laura, following Jason across the white painted boards. And how had Alec Cowray accomplished so much in such a short space of time?

'Is everything satisfactory, Mr Montefiore?' inquired one of the stewards politely, while his companion subjected Laura to an intent scrutiny. Laura had never seen either of them before, but she could guess what they were thinking. In her cheap pants and shirt and without any make-up, she was not at all the glamorous kind of female they were no doubt used to seeing. Had Alec Cowray filled them in on her previous relationship with Jason, she wondered. She didn't know which was worse: the idea that they knew she had once been Jason's mistress, or their avid speculation that she might be hoping to assume that role.

'This is fine, thank you,' Jason was saying now, his smile perfunctory but polite. He waited until Laura had taken the chair the steward held out for her before dismissing a similar attention and taking his own seat. 'We'll serve ourselves,' he added, his crisp tone tempered by his manner, and the two men departed, evidently disappointed that their services were no longer required.

A prawn cocktail, arranged on pink-fleshed bases of papaya, had been served as an appetizer, and although Laura had not felt hungry when she sat down, the sun and the breeze, and the succulent aroma of the food were seductive. While Jason was uncorking the bottle of champagne, she took a spoonful of the juicy concoction, and it was so delicious that she took another. There were warm rolls, wrapped in a cloth and residing in a basket, and creamy curls of butter, cool on a bed of ice. With a feeling of resignation, she gave in to the temptation to taste the bread, too, and by the time her glass was filled with the effervescing liquid, she was actually enjoying her meal.

Jason, she noticed, ate little, and she was relieved to see he was not drinking much either. He seemed quite content to lounge in his seat, set at right angles to hers, playing with the stem of his wine glass and watching the antics of a pair of dinghies, tacking backwards and forwards across the blue expanse of Mamala Bay.

The stewards appeared briefly to clear away the dishes already used and to set two silver-domed tureens before them. Inside, Laura discovered two whole lobsters, halved and filled with a delicious thermidor sauce, with tempting mounds of saffron rice to accompany them. 'Help yourself,' advised Jason, offering her the serving tools, and with a little sigh, she lifted half a lobster on to her plate.

'Do you want some?' she asked nervously, feeling obliged to make the gesture, and he inclined his head.

'Thank you,' he said, allowing her to serve him also, and in spite of her apprehension, she managed not to spill any in his lap.

Forking a white piece of lobster meat into her mouth, she eventually said quietly, 'Don't you think this has gone far enough?' She paused, and then added tensely, 'You don't really expect me to move back into your apartment, do you? I mean—why would you want me to? There are plenty of other women who would be only too—'

'I don't want *plenty* of other women,' retorted Jason smoothly, laying his fork aside. 'I want you.' He met her eyes squarely, and she was jolted by the unguarded passion in the depths of his. 'I'm being very civilised about this, Laura, because I sense that if I move too fast I'll have you running scared. But don't doubt my determination. It's there. Believe me!'

She did. With her throat closing up suffocatingly, she found her appetite which had flowered so unexpectedly, closing up too. 'But why?' she demanded imploringly. '*Why*?'

Jason did not dignify her plea with a reply. 'I don't live in an apartment any more, Laura,' he replied, pouring more champagne into her glass. 'I have a house, approximately two hundred and fifty miles from here, on an island called Kaulanai.'

Laura stared at him. 'Kaulanai?' she shook her head. 'I've never heard of it.'

'You wouldn't have.' Jason's expression was indifferent. 'It's only a small island. Approximately fourteen miles long by seven miles across. But it's beautiful. And it belongs to me.'

'To you?' Laura's tongue circled her dry lips. 'It's your island?'

'For my sins,' agreed Jason wryly. 'You would agree with that, I assume.'

Laura's hands curled together in her lap. 'And—and you expect me to live there?'

'Not all the time,' he assured her drily. 'I still own the apartment New York, and I keep a suite in one of the hotels here in Honolulu always available.'

Laura took a trembling breath. 'And what is your plan for Pamela? An expensive abortion?'

'Of course not.' Jason's tone hardened in response to her sarcasm. 'Though if that's what she wants, it can be arranged.' He paused. 'But no. Your sister losing her baby was not part of my plan. I'm quite prepared to support her as well as you.'

Laura shook her head. 'She'll never agree.'

'Won't she?' Jason put his glass aside and rested his elbow on the table, supporting his chin on his palm. 'Right now, Pamela is alone and desperate. She has no job and she has no money…'

'How do you know she has no job? Mrs Goldstein hasn't fired her. Pamela's a good physiotherapist…'

'I'm sure she is.' Jason shrugged. 'However, an attempted suicide is not something easy to live down. And this Mrs Goldstein, did you say? She's unlikely to want to go on employing someone with such…psychological tendencies.'

'You make her sound like a mental case!'

'No. I'm only saying she may find it difficult to take up where she left off, even should she want to. And you yourself suggested persuading her to go back to London.'

Laura sighed. 'All right. So she's in a difficult situation. I know that.'

Jason abandoned his confiding stance and lay back in his chair again. 'Okay. So we agree on something,' he remarked drily. 'Let me put it to you that your sister would find life far more appealing without any money worries, without any responsibilities—except to look after herself and be happy. And you have to admit, the climate here is a little more appealing than London.'

Laura's palms felt damp and she rubbed them hastily over the knees of her pants. 'You're suggesting we both live in your house on Kaulanai?'

Jason's lips twisted. 'Well—not quite as it sounds,' he commented sardonically. 'And I shall require you to do a little more than—*live* in my house.'

Laura trembled. 'You're disgusting!'

Jason shrugged, his expression sobering once again. 'We'll see,' he said flatly. 'Well? Is it a deal? Or are you still going to insist on flying back to San Francisco tonight?'

Laura pushed back her chair and got to her feet. 'You're crazy!'

'Am I?' Jason lifted one shoulder. 'I thought it was an eminently sane solution to your problems.'

'To Pamela's problems, perhaps!' Laura was bitter. Even in her distressed state, she could see the advantages for her sister. 'And what happens after the baby is born?'

Jason expelled his breath carelessly. 'That's for her to decide. She can always find another job, here in Hawaii. There are plenty of rich old ladies, one of whom is bound to need a personal physiotherapist.' He paused. 'I might even employ her myself.'

'You!' Laura was contemptuous.

'Why not?' Jason looked up at her levelly. 'A hotel could do worse than employ a house masseuse.'

Laura blinked. 'You own a hotel?'

'I took over the Ridgeway complex, remember?' Jason reminded her expressionlessly, and she wondered how she could ever have forgotten.

With a little shake of her head, she moved to the rail, resting her elbows upon it and gazing out across the water. Dear God, she thought despairingly, what was she going to do? He was right. He was not forcing her to do anything, not physically at least. But he was putting the whole responsibility for Pamela's happiness on her shoulders, and if anything should go wrong…

The brush of his sleeve against her bare arm made her shudderingly aware he had come to stand beside her. The heat of his flesh burning, even through the texture of his shirt, startled her into an involuntary movement away from him, but his fingers curving over the fine structure of her shoulders arrested her.

'Is it such a hard decision to make?' he murmured, the warmth of his breath against her ear, revealing he had bent his head towards her. 'You've lost weight,' he added inconsequently, feeling the fragility of the bones beneath his hand, and just for a moment she gave in to the urge to say what she was really thinking.

'So have you,' she countered, turning her head to look at him, only to discover his face was only inches from hers.

'I've missed you,' he told her huskily, the flavour of his breath, lightly scented with alcohol, not unpleasant to her nostrils. The pale gold beauty of his eyes was very disturbing, and she felt her resistance ebbing beneath that sensual appraisal. It reminded her of mornings she had wakened to find him propped on his elbow gazing down at her, and the subsequent aftermath of his possession. It reminded her of the sexual pleasure he had given her—the pleasure they had given one another— but it also occurred to her to wonder, with a shrinking heart, how many women he had pleasured since she had been gone, and that brought her to her senses.

Jerking her head away from him, she exclaimed chokingly, 'I haven't missed you!' And, less truthfully: 'I haven't thought about you at all. I enjoy my work, and I was enjoying my life, until your brother-in-law got Pamela into this mess! I've been happy these past three years. However hard that may be for you to believe!'

'Oh, I believe it!' he responded harshly, putting some space between them, and she felt an unwilling sense of deprivation at the loss. 'And I could add that your sister might be equally to blame for this mess, as you put it! However, that is not at issue here. What is, is what you are going to do about it. Have you come to a decision?'

Laura caught her breath. 'How can I?'

'What do you mean?'

'Jason, I have a job in London...'

'I know that.'

'...and...and Pierce won't keep it open for me.'

'Why should he?' Jason was suddenly very still. 'You won't be going back. At least not in the foreseeable future.'

As he spoke, he looped one arm over the rail, and her eyes were drawn to the sweat-moistened muscles of his midriff, bared by the careless opening of his shirt. And it was as if that negligent gesture crystallised in Laura's mind all that he expected of her. It was one thing to remember the way it used to be between them—the urgent, powerful emotions he had aroused so easily, his hungry passionate possession of her body. She had been in love with him then; what they had done had been the irresistible result of their need for one another. The rights and wrongs of their relationship hadn't seemed to matter. He had wanted her, and she would have done anything to please him...

But not now. Now, what they were really discussing

was a subtle kind of revenge he was going to exact upon her. For three years, he had waited for such an opportunity, and she—fool that she was—had inadvertently given it to him. She couldn't believe he cared about her, and he certainly didn't care about Pamela. He just wanted to prove he was still her master.

Pursing her lips, she said brokenly, 'You can't do this to me!'

Jason shrugged. 'I'm not doing anything to you, Laura. It's your decision. You must choose.'

'Between the serpent and the staff?' she demanded painfully. 'It's not much of a choice, is it?'

'Is that how I really appear to you?' he mused softly. 'A serpent?' He made a dismissing gesture and walked back to the table. 'Very well. I'll give you until tonight to think over what I have said.' He emptied the remains of the champagne into his glass and raised it to his lips. 'I'll 'phone you at eight o'clock precisely. Be there!'

CHAPTER FOUR

'FASTEN YOUR seat belt, Miss Huyton. We'll be landing in fifteen minutes.'

The voice of Clark Sinclair, the co-pilot of Jason's Learjet spoke to her as if from a distance, and Laura dragged her thoughts back to the present to acknowledge his instruction.

'Thank-you,' she said gratefully, feeling down the sides of the comfortable leather armchair for the meshed straps. 'I was miles away. I'm sorry.' She looked up into his fair good-looking face. 'Did you want something else?'

'Just to ask if you'd enjoyed the flight,' he responded easily, squatting down beside her. 'I guess you're going to be pretty tired this morning. Hawaiian time it's just approaching midnight.'

Laura forced a smile and nodded. 'It's been a long flight. When I flew out, I spent a few days in San Francisco.'

'Yes.' Clark evidently knew about that. 'A twenty-four hour stopover is not the same, I know. You should have gone to bed like Julie suggested. A couple of sleeping tablets, and you wouldn't have noticed the distance.'

Laura shook her head, making some deprecating comment. She could hardly tell Clark Sinclair that the reason she had not used the luxurious sleeping compartment of the aircraft was because, like so many other things, it brought back memories of sharing it with Jason. Time enough to think of those things when she was on her way back to Hawaii. Right now, she faced the prospect of telling Pierce of her decision, and the poignant task of closing up her flat and handing over the keys to some-one else.

The sleek executive jet landed at Gatwick, and the customs formalities were soon dealt with. The fact that Laura was a returning British national made her entry simple, and after arranging the details of the return flight with the pilot, Frank Danielli, she wished the three mem-bers of the crew goodbye, and took a train into the city.

London was reassuringly familiar, although she felt a distinct sense of chill after the warmth of Hawaii. April was not the most predictable month in England, and she was not surprised to see specks of rain against the train's windows as they pulled into Victoria station. She emerged from the station, hailed a taxi and told the driver to take her directly to Highgate. She knew she was putting off the moment when she would have to speak to Pierce. It hardly seemed possible it was little more than a week since she had left him. Her whole life had been altered since she flew almost blithely out of Heathrow, *en route* for San Francisco.

The flat felt chilled when she opened the door, even though the heating was run from a central generator. In her absence, no one had turned the thermostat up, and she guessed it confirmed her theory that spring had not truly arrived yet. There were letters in her small lobby, bills for the most part, and she realised that was some-thing else she would have to deal with. She would ar-range with the post office to have her mail sent on at regular intervals. There was not likely to be much. Apart from a few odd aunts and cousins here and there, the two girls had no close surviving relatives.

Examining the contents of the fridge, Laura found an

unopened carton of milk and filled the kettle to make herself some tea. It was strange to think that if she had still been in Hawaii, she would be in bed at this moment. Clark was right; it was disorientating; but she had made the transition one way, she could make it the other.

While she drank her tea, she flicked through the mail, setting the bills aside for immediate payment. Apart from an invitation to a party, being given by one of Pierce's friends, and several envelopes containing advertising, there was nothing of any interest, and she eventually pushed the clutter aside and rested her chin on her upturned palms.

She had a week, that was all, a week to tie up the ends of her life here and fly back to California. By then, Pamela would be ready to accompany her to Hawaii, and together they would make the comparatively short trip to Kaulanai.

The island was some two thousand miles off the American mainland, two hundred and fifty miles southeast of Oahu. According to Jason, it could only be reached commercially from the air, a telling factor she was sure when he first considered its advantages. A reef surrounded it on all sides, only negotiable at high tide by craft with a very shallow draught. Certainly, the *Laura M* could never navigate the reef, and it provided a natural barrier to any would-be intruder.

Not that Laura had been particularly interested in his description of the island. So far as she was concerned, Kaulanai was fast assuming the proportions of a prison, and the fact that there were no bars, did not make it any less confining. Just because Pamela had reacted to Jason's offer with the first trace of animation she had shown since Laura had found her, unconscious in the flat, did not make what she was doing any easier. She felt bruised and resentful, and totally incapable of accepting his aspirations for her future.

Pierce was equally appalled at her decision. 'You can't be serious!' he exclaimed, the silver cigarette holder, which he used as an affectation, falling unheeded to the carpet. Putting the cigarette he had been about to light between his lips, he gazed at her disbelievingly. 'My dear girl, I know I may have been a bit miffed at you swanning off like that, and maybe I was a little too forthright in my objections, but surely you know I have great respect for you, as a person! I don't want to lose you, Laura. There—now you've really got me over a barrel!'

Laura shook her head, sinking down into the chintz-covered armchair at one side of the elegant marble fireplace. She knew Pierce's house almost as well as her own home, and she had often stayed in his spare room after working with him long into the night. Often Pierce's best inspiration had come after darkness had fallen, and she had enjoyed their midnight sessions, and the sense of chill his books always evoked.

'I'm sorry,' she said now, as he took the seat opposite her, coiling his long angular frame into the chair. 'It's not something I want to do. It's something I *have* to do, for Pamela. I can't explain exactly, but—well, she needs me and I can't let her down.'

'You're telling me your sister needs a nursemaid?' demanded Pierce uncomprehendingly, lighting his cigarette and inhaling the nicotine deep into his lungs. 'But I thought she was only two years younger than you are.'

'She is.' Laura sighed. 'Oh, that's not the only reason I'm staying. Don't ask me to explain, Pierce. It's a long story, and you wouldn't want to hear it.'

'Try me.'

Laura bent her head. 'Please. I can't go through all that now. If I say there's a man—a man I used to—work for, when I lived in Honolulu, will you try to understand? He...well, he's offered to help Pamela, providing I'm prepared to...to help him.'

'Work for him, you mean?' Pierce stared at her blankly, and Laura was glad of the heat of the fire to disguise her burning cheeks.

'Yes,' she answered now, seizing the reprieve. 'I was his secretary for a time. The fact that I can speak several languages was an advantage to him.'

'Really?' Pierce regarded her suspiciously. 'Are you telling me there are no linguists in Hawaii? I can't believe it.'

'No, I'm not saying that.' Laura shifted uncomfortably. 'Pierce, Jason—Mr Montefiore, that is—has made my...*employment* a condition of his helping Pamela.'

'How is he helping Pamela exactly?'

'I've told you.' Laura hesitated. 'He's allowing her to stay in the islands until she's had the baby. Then it's up to her.'

Pierce absorbed this silently for a few moments. Then, he said quietly, 'So in what—nine months, maybe less, you'll be free to return to England?'

Laura frowned. 'I suppose so.' She blinked. That thought hadn't occurred to her. Once her sister had had her baby, Jason would have no further hold over her. Surely by then Pamela's mental condition would no longer be a cause for concern.

'Very well, then.' Pierce exhaled blue smoke into the air above their heads. 'If you insist on sacrificing yourself like this, I'll just have to find myself a *temporary* replacement.'

'Temporary?' Laura stared at him.

'Why not?' Pierce shrugged indifferently. 'Having just initiated you into my ways, I am not attracted by the notion of having to repeat the exercise. No. The new book must be completed, of course. That goes without saying. But once that is done, I am thinking of taking a break—somewhere like India, perhaps. Or the Far East. I've got an urge to see Singapore and Hong Kong. I was going to suggest that you came with me, to make notes, that sort of thing. But I suppose I can record my impressions on tape, for you to transcribe when you get back.'

'Oh, Pierce!' Laura was touched. 'I don't know what to say.'

'Say nothing, my dear. That's always the best way. Who knows, you may decide to stay with your Mr Montefiore, and I shouldn't like you to commit yourself without first considering all the facts.'

Laura pressed her lips together. 'I don't think that's likely.'

'Don't you?' Pierce's grey eyes were disturbingly shrewd. 'I wish I could be as confident. I'm afraid age, and experience, have made me wary.'

Nevertheless, it was a reassurance in the hectic days that followed, for Laura to know she was not severing all ties with England. She had to give up her flat, of course. She could not afford to pay the cost of renting and heating four rooms when she was not using them, but it had been a furnished flat, after all, and she could hopefully find another on her return. The belongings she would not be taking with her, Pierce agreed to store in the basement of his house in Eaton Terrace, and her mail was to be redirected there for his housekeeper to send on.

'You've been so kind,' Laura told him, the night before she was due to leave for San Francisco. For once, Pierce had invited her out for dinner, and they were seated at a table for two in the rather plush surroundings of his club. 'You've made everything so much easier. I almost feel I'm not making a break at all. Just taking a sort of...leave of absence.'

'That's what I want you to think,' declared Pierce firmly, pushing his horn-rimmed spectacles over the bridge of his nose. 'You know, Laura, I've never said this to any woman before, but if I ever thought of marrying, it would be someone like you.'

Laura smiled. The image of the fastidious and aristocratic Pierce Carver in the role of husband and father was not one she could easily summon. At forty-three years of age, he had always struck her as the quintessential bachelor, and she had never regarded him as anything more than a friend.

'You're very gallant,' she murmured now, pushing the fillet steak she had ordered round her plate, in an effort for it to appear that she was eating it. 'But I'm sure if you ever do decide to sacrifice your freedom, you'll find someone infinitely more suitable to share your life.'

'What you mean is—you don't see me as the man in your life,' Pierce amended drily. 'I know you weren't fishing for compliments, my dear, but I'll offer you one just the same. A man could do much worse than choose you for his wife, Laura. You're a beautiful woman— no!' this as she would have contradicted him; 'I mean it. Beauty isn't only a thing of the body, although I have to say, your appearance gives me much pleasure. It's also a thing of the soul, of the inner you, of the person you are inside. And you're a beautiful person, Laura. I've always thought so.'

'Oh, Pierce...'

Laura gazed at him helplessly, and he stretched out a hand to touch her cheek. 'I know,' he said. 'I've waited too long to tell you. I realised that the minute you told me you were flying out to San Francisco because your sister had 'phoned you. I wanted to tell you then, but I couldn't, so I behaved quite abominably, I don't deny it.' He shrugged. 'Don't look so worried, my dear. I'm not about to threaten some dire consequence if you can't return my feelings. I fear I'm too selfish a person for that. But I shall miss you, remember that, and if you need me, I'll always be here.'

'Thank you.'

Laura was overwhelmed, and she was grateful for the advent of the waiter to lighten their mood. She had never dreamt Pierce might be harbouring any feelings for her, and she thought how ironic it was that Jason should have been proved right, at least in one respect.

The unwilling reminder of why she and Pierce were having this dinner together was not welcome. For the past days, she had been struggling to keep thoughts of Jason from intruding on her daytime hours, and although she had not entirely succeeded, only at night had she truly given way to her latent fears and apprehensions. She was sleeping badly, and her appetite was practically non-existent, and now the involuntary invasion of his image into this most-poignant of occasions was almost overwhelming. She was tempted to confide in Pierce; she was tempted to tell him what she was doing, and let him solve the problem for her, but she couldn't. She didn't love him, and it wouldn't be fair to put that burden on him. The fact that she didn't love Jason either, she dismissed. After all, she told herself defensively, if it hadn't been for Jason's brother-in-law, she wouldn't be in the position she was in now.

The meal was over and they were enjoying a liqueur with their coffee, when Laura became conscious of a sense of unease, of a disturbing awareness that she was being observed, and immediately she thought of Jason's private investigator. But he would not have engaged anyone to watch her during this short visit to London, she told herself firmly. With Pamela still in San Francisco, he could have no fears that she might not return.

Nevertheless, the feeling persisted, and lifting her head, she gazed dubiously about the room. Which of these rather distinguished-looking gentlemen was likely to be employed as a private investigator, she mused, fighting back the urge to ask Pierce if they could go. It was stupid, and she was probably imagining the whole thing, but she sensed a growing hostility, and she couldn't help associating it with her reluctant thoughts of Jason.

And as if thinking of him had conjured the man himself, it was at that moment she saw him, seated at the bar only thirty feet away. He was occupying one of the tall stools that flanked the curved counter, but he was half turned in his seat so that he could watch her, and she had no doubt now that he had been responsible for her sudden distress. In a wine-coloured velvet dinner jacket and tight-fitting black pants, he looked unusually sombre, the pleated front of his shirt contrasting sharply with the darkness of his skin. He was resting one elbow on the bar, beside the half-filled tumbler of what she assumed to be scotch that marked his place, and although one foot was hooked on the rail of the stool the other rested on the floor. His attitude tautened the flow of cloth across his thighs, drawing her attention to the muscled strength of his legs. His expression was not friendly; even when he met her shocked gaze there was no trace of recognition in his. On the contrary, she thought he was going to ignore her, and her mouth dried with the anticipation of wondering what he intended to do.

'Is something wrong?'

Pierce had noticed her unusual stillness, the sudden draining of colour from her face, and Laura struggled to recover her equilibrium. 'Not…exactly,' she murmured, looking down at the coffee in her cup. 'I…the man I'm going to work for in Hawaii has just come in. I didn't expect to see him, that all.'

'Montefiore? He's here!'

Pierce had noticed the direction of her gaze, and now he turned in his seat to stare frowningly across the room. Laura wanted to stop him, but she didn't know how she could, and when she ventured a fleeting glance towards the bar, she saw Jason sliding indolently from the stool to stroll towards them.

'That's him? That's Montefiore?' whispered Pierce, leaning towards her with some surprise, and Laura nodded. 'But I thought…I assumed he'd be older—' Pierce broke off in evident confusion. 'What is he doing here? Do you know?'

'I've no idea,' replied Laura in a low voice, just as Jason reached their table, and it was with a distinct effort she raised her eyes to his. 'Hello, Jason,' she greeted him stiffly. 'This is…unexpected.'

'Hello, Laura.' Jason had pushed his hands into two pockets that followed the waistband of his pants in front. The action pushed the sides of his jacket aside, exposing the width of his chest and the muscled contours of his thighs. It was a deliberate attitude he had adopted, she felt, his manner bordering on the insolent, and when she introduced Pierce, he shook the other man's hand with only perfunctory courtesy.

'You're in London on business, Mr Montefiore?' inquired Pierce politely, somewhat at a disadvantage when Jason waived his attempt to get to his feet.

'In a manner of speaking,' Jason responded smoothly, his expression giving nothing away. 'I understand you're a writer, Mr Carver.'

'I like to think so.' Pierce gave Laura a reassuring smile. 'Does your presence in London mean Miss Huyton will not be required to return to Hawaii immediately? If so...'

'I shall be returning to the west coast tomorrow,' Jason interrupted him swiftly, intercepting Laura's gaze and holding it with cold deliberation. 'I thought we might travel back together, Miss Huyton. That is, if you have no objection to that arrangement.'

'Of course not.' How could she have? Laura thought desperately, gazing up at him in pained resentment. Couldn't he at least have allowed her these last few days of freedom? Had he made the sixteen hour trip to London, just to ensure she didn't change her mind?

Pierce was watching their exchange with frowning speculation, and Laura guessed he was wondering exactly what it meant. However, good manners prevented him from voicing his feelings, and instead he invited Jason to join them for a drink.

'I'm afraid I can't.' Jason's refusal was tempered by a thin smile, and Laura expelled her breath on a trembling sigh, hardly aware until that moment she had been holding it. Let him go! she begged silently, all too conscious of his leg only inches away from her own. In spite of her hatred for him, she could not ignore him, and she was uncomfortably aware of the effect he was having on her.

Surreptitiously, she smoothed her damp palms on her linen napkin, keeping it well below the level of the table as she did so. But she could not slow the erratic thumping of her heart, or cool the burning temperature of her blood. It was incredibly difficult not to compare the two men, and against Pierce's bony angularity, Jason's decidedly sexual indolence was markedly pronounced. It was not a conscious thing with him; it was simply a matter of taste; but Laura could not deny the unholy attraction of a lithe, powerful body and features as arrogant as the devil's himself.

'As a matter of fact, I was wondering whether you would have any objections to my taking Miss Huyton home,' Jason continued now, stunning Laura by his audacity. 'I need to speak with her before tomorrow, and as we have had the good fortune to run into one another...'

Pierce was taken aback. 'I—well—if you think... Laura, what have you to say?' he faltered, evidently at a loss for words, and Jason turned to her with unconcealed impatience.

Laura didn't know what to say. She didn't believe Jason's remark about running into one another. It was too much of a coincidence. But on the other hand, how could she refuse him, without some reasonable excuse?

'Couldn't we talk here?' she asked, meeting Jason's pale eyes and shivering at the implacability she read there.

'I'd prefer to speak to you in private, Laura,' he essayed politely, and only she was aware of the inflexibility of his words.

'I—well, would you mind, Pierce?' she murmured unhappily, and he had little choice but to give his permission.

'If…if you have no objections, my dear,' he declared regretfully, and she wondered what he would say if she told him she had as little enthusiasm for the motion as he had.

It was hard saying goodbye with Jason looking on. 'Remember what I told you,' Pierce reminded her huskily, when he drew her close for moment and bestowed a warm kiss on her temple. 'I'll always be here, if you need me.'

'I'll remember,' said Laura tremulously. 'Take care.'

'And you,' added Pierce gruffly, and without looking at Jason again, Laura walked blindly away from both of them.

She was collecting her coat from the cloakroom when Jason joined her. 'Ready?' he inquired tautly, without really requiring a reply. Instead, he turned away to inform the doorman they were leaving, and by the time Laura had slipped her cape about her shoulders, a taxi was waiting for them. 'Shall I give your address or will you come back to my hotel?' he asked her carelessly as they descended the steps into Jermyn Street, and Laura thought how arrogant he was to assume that either alternative would please her.

'I'd prefer to go home,' she declared tightly, and it was only as he climbed into the back of the cab beside her that the significance of his having her address occurred to her. 'How did you know where I lived?' she exclaimed, as he flung himself on to the hard leather seat beside her, and he cast a shadowed glance in her direction.

'Think about it,' he advised drily, and she wondered

how she could have forgotten his humiliating surveillance.

'Wh—what did you want to talk to me about?' she demanded gathering the folds of her cloak about her.

'Later,' he responded without emotion, and her resentment grew at his deliberate insolence.

'It wasn't a coincidence, was it?' she exclaimed fiercely. 'Your being at Pierce's club. You're not a member of that club, are you? You came there looking for me!'

'For both of you,' offered Jason coolly. 'The stalwart British novelist and his oh-so-conscientious secretary!'

'What is that supposed to mean?'

'You weren't taking dictation this evening, Laura!'

'No.' She held up her head. 'We were having dinner together. What's wrong with that?'

Jasons eyes were turned on her, and although she couldn't see their expression, she could sense their hostility. 'Do you often have dinner with your—*employer*?'

'Not often, no...'

'I'll bet.' Jason's tone was contemptuous, and Laura gazed at him frustratedly.

'What are you implying?' she demanded. 'I told you. Pierce and I are friends...'

'And that, I suppose, is why he was holding your hand and stroking your cheek,' he remarked grimly, and Laura gasped.

'You were watching us!'

'Long enough,' he agreed, returning his attention to the lighted façade of a cinema they were passing.

'You—you bastard...'

'Don't call me names, Laura,' he advised her bleakly, keeping his eyes on the road. 'I may reciprocate in kind, and you wouldn't like it.'

Laura trembled. 'Do you know how much I hate you?'

'I can live with it.'

'You're going to have to!'

'Yes, I am, aren't I?' he countered mockingly, and her chest heaved with the realisation that he meant every word he said.

When they reached the small square where Laura had her flat, she half hoped he would leave her there. He had achieved his objective, after all, she thought bitterly. He had taken her away from Pierce, he had already exerted his authority, and she didn't see what else he could have to say. But as she thrust open her door and scrambled out, she heard him asking the driver how much he wanted, and the cab drove away leaving Jason on the pavement.

'Number 47, isn't that right?' he inquired flatly, his hand gripping her upper arm compelling her into the building, and she expelled her breath wearily.

The bare tiled floor was much different from the carpeted corridors he was used to, she reflected, as they crossed the entrance hall and entered the lift. The metal cubicle was uninviting, too, with its scrawled graffiti and faint aroma of pine disinfectant.

Laura's flat was on the fourth level. The ground floor of the building counted as the first to simplify the numbering system, and it took little time to reach her floor. The lift doors slid back on a narrow corridor without warmth or character, and she hoped Jason was already regretting his decision to accompany her inside. Not that he seemed overly concerned. He followed her along the rubber tiled hallway to her door without any obvious sign of distaste, but she guessed he was an adept at hiding his true feelings.

The living room of the flat looked bare and uninviting,

too. With her small collection of books and ornaments already packed and waiting for transportation to Eaton Terrace, the place looked as impersonal as an hotel room. Halting in the middle of the floor, she was struck once again by the ignominy of her position, and her shoulders sagged in an attitude of helpless defeat.

'How long have you lived here?' asked Jason quietly, as if perceiving her desperation, and she struggled to keep a sense of perspective.

'Al...almost three years,' she got out unsteadily. 'When I—when I came back from—from Hawaii, a friend of Pamela's was just moving out. I was lucky enough to be offered it.'

'When you came back from Hawaii,' echoed Jason softly, and she wished she had not chosen that particular point of contact. 'It's been a long time, Laura,' he added, and although she had not been aware of his stepping towards her, his breath was now warm against her cheek.

'Not long enough,' she choked, and would have stepped away from him, but he grasped the epaulette of her cloak to keep her beside him.

'Don't fight me, Laura,' he advised her harshly, and she shivered again at the threatening note in his voice. 'I don't want to hurt you, but I should warn you, I'm finding it increasingly difficult to keep this conversation on a civil basis!'

'Is that what you think you're doing?' With desperation spilling over into reckless defiance, Laura whirled away from him, the cloak slipping from her shoulders as she did so. 'How could you be civil, Jason? You're not a civilised person! You're a savage! A barbarian! A man who doesn't hesitate to use other people's pain and misery to gain his own ends!'

'Be careful, Laura!' Jason was standing very still, the

superfluous folds of her cloak still hanging uselessly from his hand, but she was beyond restraint.

'Be careful!' she mocked him. 'Why should I be careful? When has *being careful* helped me? I thought I was being careful when I came back to England. I thought leaving you was the *careful* thing to do. But I was wrong, wasn't I? You know, it has crossed my mind that perhaps you put Mike Kazantis up to having an affair with Pamela! How convenient that would have been for you, wouldn't it?'

In fact, until that moment, such a notion had not crossed Laura's mind, and as soon as the words were uttered, she thought how ludicrous they were. Even if Jason had welcomed Pamela's association with his sister's husband, which was unlikely, how could he have known Pamela would get pregnant? Or indeed that such a circumstance would force her into trying to take her own life!

But the words were said, and before she could take them back, Jason's patience snapped. Tossing the cloak aside, he crossed the thin expanse of carpet that separated them, and took her shoulders in a bruising grip. 'If you believe that, why should I disappoint you?' he said grimly, jerking her towards him. 'As you appear to regard me as the devil incarnate, I might as well take advantage of the fact. It isn't as if it hasn't been in my mind, ever since I saw you by the pool at the Kapulani.'

In spite of her hands crushed between them, his mouth ground down on hers without impediment, and she tasted her own blood on her tongue. He was so much stronger than she was, so much more powerful, and the violence of his action rendered any real resistance unviable. He was not wearing any overcoat and his unbuttoned jacket meant she was that much closer to him. Her knuckles dug into the muscled flatness of his stomach, and her knees bumped the unyielding hardness of his legs. She was enveloped in the heat and scent and feel of him, and although she fought against it, his sexuality was quite insidious.

'Jason, *for God's sake*—' she gasped chokingly, when he released her mouth to seek the exposed hollow of her shoulder, but her pleas were all in vain.

'Why appeal to that divine deity, when you believe I'm the seed of a lower order?' he taunted harshly, forcing the draped neckline of her simple black cocktail dress down off her shoulders and tearing the cloth in the process. 'You asked for this, Laura. I was prepared to be patient with you, but you changed the rules of the game.' His teeth skimmed her skin, and the nerves so near the surface palpitated wildly. 'Don't complain now, if your opponent stoops to cheating!'

'Jason, you can't do this!' she moaned, feeling the soft folds of the dress pooling around her ankles. She was vulnerable now, standing there before him in only a lacy waist slip and camisole, and although she made the protest, she had little hope of its being fulfilled.

'I can, and I must,' he told her thickly, his tawny eyes raking her slim figure with burning intensity. With one hand at her nape, holding her easily within his grasp, his free hand groped for his tie and the tiny concealed buttons beneath the pleating of his shirt. But his efforts were too slow and growing impatient with the task, he tore his shirt open, exposing the brown expanse of his chest.

Then, as if desperate to touch her, he dragged her close against him, and even through the satin camisole she could feel the taut abrasion of the hair that arrowed down to his navel and beyond.

'You have no idea how much I want you,' he muttered, his tongue making its own possession, and a dizzying feeling of weakness swept over her. His lips were gentler now, almost sensually persuasive, and when his fingers slipped beneath the hem of the camisole and spread against the fragile hollow of her spine, she felt an involuntary shudder of desire.

With his mouth still on hers, he pressed the straps of her camisole down off her shoulders, and her breasts emerged to thrust against his bared chest. Just for a moment, he held her against him again, his hands on her hips hard through the thinness of her slip and panties. But the swollen ridge of muscle riding up between them demanded release, and with a muffled oath, he shrugged off his jacket and shirt and swung her up into his arms.

He seemed to know instinctively which door led to her bedroom, and although he put no lights on, the illumination spilling from the living room behind them showed him the narrow outline of her single bed. With infinite indulgence, he laid her on the bed, and even though in some distant corner of her mind a small voice was screaming at her to escape now, when she had the chance, she lay open-mouthed watching Jason strip the rest of his clothes from his body.

It was only when the pulsating proof of his maleness was exposed that she knew a momentary sense of panic. But before the realisation that neither of them was taking any precautions could evoke any positive action from her, he was beside her on the bed, and the hungry pressure of his mouth made any resistance impossible.

'Don't fight me,' he breathed against her lips, his fingers disposing of the flimsy shreds of fabric that still separated them, and Laura trembled beneath the probing intimacy of his hands. No man had touched her since her reckless flight from the man who was touching her now, and in spite of their previous relationship, she felt as tense and sensitive as if she had not once known Jason's body as well as her own. 'You're so beautiful,' he groaned, lowering his head to her taut nipples and suckling from each of them in turn, and Laura's breathing felt suspended as she watched his dark head moving against her breast. Almost without volition, her hands came up to tangle in the silky smoothness of his hair, and he shifted sensuously against her, letting her feel his throbbing need.

'Relax,' he whispered, moving over her, and her legs fell apart so that his hardness nudged her with sensual arousal.

It was almost like the first time he had made love to her, except that this time she knew what to expect. The temporary discomfort of his entry was quickly dispelled by the liquid response of her senses to his undeniable attraction. And Jason's murmured, 'So there has been no one else!' was only a momentary irritation as her tender muscles opened to his urgent penetration. The seductive caress of his tongue was making rational thought an effort, and in spite of her mental opposition to his arrogant appropriation of her life, her body seemed to have a will of its own. Her limbs wrapped themselves about him eagerly, as if welcoming his invasion, and when he moved against her, she couldn't prevent her involuntary response.

He possessed her passionately, his muscles thrusting urgently into her, his quickening breath only matching her own for fervency. She couldn't see his face, but she could feel the sweat on his forehead when he buried his face in her neck, moistening the strands of hair that had broken loose from her braid, cooling on her flesh as he lifted himself above her.

It was all over quite quickly. Although Jason would evidently have liked to prolong his pleasure, his need was too great, and Laura felt the quivering delight released within her only seconds before Jason flooded her with his warmth. He slumped against her, shuddering in the aftermath of his emotion, and although she knew she ought to push him away, she was too languorously content to do it...

CHAPTER FIVE

LAURA HAD BEEN working in the Honolulu office less than two weeks when she first met Jason Montefiore.

As a newcomer, her initial duties had kept her employed within the agency itself, and the novelty of living and working in such exotic surroundings was such, she had not yet started envying the other girls when they were sent out on assignments to clients on Oahu, and to other islands in the group. Sharing a flat with two other employees of the agency near the Moanalua golf course, she was quite content to spend her days answering the 'phone and attending to client's queries, when in the evenings and at weekends she could swim and sunbathe and enjoy all the other delights that the island had to offer.

She soon made friends with her colleagues, and the one thing she did envy was their natural resistance to the sun's rays. Her own skin was so fair, she had to avoid over-exposure, and she despaired of ever achieving the gold tan her friends took for granted. She was totally unaware of how outstanding her colouring was, or that its very individuality was extremely attractive. Instead, she persevered in her efforts to achieve her objective, suffering the pain of sun-burn with a fortitude she had not known she possessed.

By the time Lucas Kamala walked into the agency, looking for a temporary secretary for his employer, her skin had acquired the glow of pale honey; and with her silvery hair drawn back loosely from a central parting and secured at her nape with a barrette, he had been instantly intrigued by her air of cool detachment.

Paula Sylva, who ran the agency in Honolulu, had not been enthusiastic about assigning Laura to this particular client. Jason Montefiore's name was not unknown in the islands, and she would have preferred to send one of her more experienced secretaries. It was the first time he had contacted the agency, and she was loath to assign someone whose experience was still confined to English ways. But, there was no one else available at that time, and Lucas Kamala was evidently prepared to employ the English girl.

For her part, Laura was delighted to be given the chance to prove herself. Paula's warning that as a representative of the agency any future employment rested in *her* hands, seemed over-dramatic, until she walked into the opulent surroundings of the Blue Orchid Club. Only then did she realise that this was no ordinary assignment, and that Jason Montefiore was probably the most influential client she was ever likely to meet.

The club itself was situated on Kapiolani Boulevard, and occupied the basement and lower floors of a skyscraper block, also owned by the Montefiore corporation. Although Laura got her first glimpse of the Blue Orchid as she accompanied Lucas Kamala through the marbled lobby of the building, Jason's office, and his apartment, were on the penthouse floor.

She remembered clearly her first interview with the owner of the Blue Orchid. When she had been shown into the office where she was to work, Jason had not been around, and Lucas Kamala had spent some time explaining where everything was, and what she was required to do.

'Mr Montefiore's secretary has broken her wrist,

windsurfing,' he replied, in answer to her instinctive
query. His eyes filled with reluctant amusement. 'You
don't windsurf, do you, Miss Huyton? Or if you do, can
I ask you to refrain from doing so until Marsha's back
on her feet?'

'I don't,' confessed Laura ruefully, examining the sophisticated word-processor with some misgivings. 'And
I have to tell you—I've never used one of these before
either. Perhaps Paula was right. Perhaps she should have
assigned one of the other girls, after all.'

'I wouldn't say that.'

The faintly mocking comment had come from somewhere behind her, and Laura had swung round to find a
man leaning against the frame of the door which led to
the inner office. In a navy blue knitted shirt, with short
sleeves and opened at the neck to expose the brown column of his throat, and matching shorts which came mid-
way down his thigh, he exuded an air of careless sexuality, that was no less potent in its casual form. That he
had been exercising, or involved in some other physical
activity, was evident in the sweat gleaming in the hollow
of his throat and moistening the dark hairs that liberally
covered his arms and legs. His hair, too, was damp
across his forehead and clung wetly to the nape of his
neck, and Laura, who had never found anything attractive in sweating bodies in the past, was instantly aware
that there were exceptions to every rule. As he stood
there, propped lazily against the frame, the heated scent
of his body came to them, but Laura found nothing to
repulse her in that distinctly masculine smell.

Even so, she had never suspected that this might be
her employer. Some relative of his perhaps, she had sur-
mised, acknowledging the fact that he had evidently entered the suite of offices through Jason Montefiore's

room. But not Montefiore himself, not the rich and powerful proprietor of the Blue Orchid Club, not the owner of the building in which they were standing. It was for this reason that she had not looked away from those lazy golden eyes or been intimidated by his decidedly insolent appraisal. She had met his gaze fearlessly, slim and golden herself, in a simple primrose-coloured island cotton, with narrow straps and an elasticated waist.

'Jase!' It was Lucas Kamala who alerted her to the man's identity, and as her eyes widened in disbelief, Jason Montefiore straightened away from the door and came indolently into his secretary's office.

'I see you found a replacement for Marsha,' he remarked, addressing his comments to Lucas, but keeping his eyes on Laura's discomfited countenance. 'Did I detect an English accent? She certainly doesn't look as if she was born in the islands.'

Resenting the fact that he was speaking of her as if she was either deaf, dumb, or both, Laura leapt to her own defence. 'I am English,' she admitted quickly. 'But the agency likes to give its employees experience in other agencies around the world, and I'm working in Honolulu for six months while someone else does my job in London.'

Jason halted in front of her, disconcerting her by his height and darkness, and by the lean muscularity of his body that much closer to her own. 'Your opposite number here, I guess,' he remarked, addressing her for the first time, and she tilted her chin determinedly, not wanting to reveal how aware of him she was.

'No,' she replied, swallowing. 'I—I believe the girl who used to work here is working in the New York office at the moment.' She flushed in spite of herself. 'It isn't as complicated as it sounds.'

'No?' Jason regarded her intently. 'So—what's your name?'

'Huyton. Laura Huyton,' said Laura hurriedly. 'But I may not be the replacement you're looking for.'

'Why not?'

'Because—I'm not used to such sophisticated machinery,' murmured Laura awkwardly, glancing round the room. 'I think perhaps you ought to contact Mrs Sylva again. She may be able to supply you with a more experienced operator.'

Jason exchanged a look with Lucas Kamala and then lifted his shoulders in a dismissing movement. 'No sweat,' he declared. 'Luke can give you any instruction that's necessary. You do type, don't you? You can use an audio machine?'

'Of course.' Laura moistened her lips.

'Okay.' Jason turned abruptly away, and strolled back towards his office. 'I need a shower. See you in fifteen minutes, Luke,' and before Laura could make any objection, the door slammed behind him.

He summoned her into his office some twenty minutes later. Sleek and darkly attractive now, in a pale grey silk suit that fitted him with the glove-like elegance of expert tailoring, he proceeded to prove why he was already a millionaire at the age of thirty-three. By the end of that day, Laura felt as limp and exhausted as a runner at the end of a marathon, whereas her employer revealed no visible strains whatsoever. On the contrary, she knew from telephone calls he had made and received in her presence that he would be spending at least part of his evening in the club downstairs, and the letters and contracts she had typed were aside from the everyday problems of the Blue Orchid.

In the days that followed, Laura learned to cope far

more quickly than she had anticipated. Lucas Kamala helped her a lot, and Jason himself was generally tolerant of her initial errors. Their relationship never quite achieved the same informality that it had on that first occasion, but he was always polite and considerate, and willing to give her time to find her feet. It was tiring work, and she seldom had time to sit back and put her feet up as she had been used to doing in the London office. But because of this, the time passed swiftly, and she looked forward to each day with growing anticipation.

Sylvie Lomax, one of the girls she shared the flat with, was the first to express any opinion about her employer. 'Better you than me, sweetie,' she remarked rather maliciously, after learning who Laura was working for. 'The man's got quite a reputation, and I don't just mean as a stud! Don't get in his way, will you? I hear he's pretty ruthless when he's crossed!'

'Isn't everybody?' Rose Cheong, the other occupant of the flat, demanded impatiently. She turned to Laura, her narrow features alight with sympathy. 'Take no notice of Sylvie. She's only jealous.'

'Jealous!' Sylvie snorted, but her expression softened when she met Laura's anxious eyes. 'Well, perhaps I am…a little,' she confessed drily. 'Though there are rumours about how he made his money, which aren't exactly savoury.'

In the weeks to come, Laura had reason to remember what Sylvie had said, at least so far as Jason's private life was concerned. She got tired of intercepting 'phone calls from females angry because he hadn't contacted them, and accepting their abuse when they refused to believe she had passed on their messages.

'It's not his fault,' Lucas assured her gently, when she

expressed her frustration to him. 'Honestly, Laura...'
they had soon progressed to first name terms '...in his
position, it's an occupational hazard! Be thankful
Regina's away in Europe at the moment. She, you might
not find so easy to handle!'

That was the first Laura had heard of Jason's ex-wife,
but eventually she learned all about the sultry Italian
model he had married when he was scarcely out of his
teens and who had divorced him less than three years
later. Despite the alimony he paid, Regina's demands on
her ex-husband, particularly financial ones were consid-
erable, and the fact their daughter, Lucia, lived with her
mother, seemed to make Jason more tolerant than he
might otherwise have been.

Laura gradually made the acquaintance of the other
members of Jason's staff. Lucas took her downstairs one
afternoon, and showed her round the luxurious nightclub, with its bars and gaming facilities, and the theatre-
restaurant, where diners were entertained by some of the
most highly-paid performers in the world. Anyone who
was anyone eventually appeared in the Pagoda Room at
the Blue Orchid, and Laura got used to seeing people
whose names were household words passing through her
office on their way to Jason's inner sanctum.

One evening, about three weeks after she had started
working for the Montefiore corporation, Jason invited
her into his sitting room for a drink. She had been working later than usual, so that Jason could finish dictating
the details of a plan for some real estate he had tendered
for. It was not the sort of thing he could consign to a
tape and he had paused every now and then to explain
certain complications to her. In consequence, it was after
seven o'clock when they finally completed the job, and

Laura was not altogether surprised by his cursory invitation.

'It's not necessary, Mr Montefiore,' she assured him firmly, getting up from her chair, and flexing her aching back muscles, and he looked up at her broodingly, his pale eyes guarded behind the fringe of his lashes.

'I know it's not,' he essayed after a moment, pushing back his own chair and standing. 'But I want to talk to you. Okay?'

Laura could think of no reason to refuse, even though her skin prickled at the thought of being alone with him in the privacy of his apartment. It was one thing to face him across the width of a desk, with the whole gamut of office protocol between them, and quite another to join him in a purely social capacity, knowing as she did how vulnerable she had felt on that other occasion.

It was her first glimpse of Jason's apartment, and she was suitably impressed. Luxuriously furnished, with wide balconies facing the ocean, it overlooked the whole curve of Waikiki, the sounds from below muted by its soaring exclusivity. Pausing by the open balcony doors, Laura could see there were still surfers lying offshore, their heads bobbing about in the water, waiting for the breakers to sweep them inward. But after dark, she guessed the view would be even more spectacular, with the colourful lights of Kalakaua Avenue gleaming like the jewels in a necklace.

'What would you like to drink?' Jason inquired behind her, and turning, Laura saw he had stepped behind a small bar, set in one corner, and generously equipped with every kind of alcohol she could think of.

'Oh—anything will do,' she murmured, not liking to ask for the cocktail she had tried on several occasions with her friends, and Jason shrugged.

'How about a pina colada?' he suggested carelessly. 'My daughter likes them a lot. It's like a Chi Chi, with rum instead of vodka.'

Laura gazed at him. 'Your daughter's only twelve, isn't she?' she asked aghast, and his lazy grin sent a quiver of unwilling excitement down her spine.

'Haven't you heard of virgin cocktails?' he asked, mixing the ingredients in a blender.

Laura shook her head. 'No.'

'Well, you have now,' he conceded lightly. 'No alcohol!'

Laura moistened her lips. 'I've never met your daughter,' she murmured, as much for something to say as anything. 'Is she like you, or—or your wife?'

'My *ex*-wife,' amended Jason evenly, the crushed ice chinking deliciously as he poured her cocktail into a tall glass. He paused to add a slice of pineapple to the side of the glass before handing it to her. 'She's one of the reasons why I wanted to speak to you.'

Laura took the glass and their fingers touched, and it was as if his skin had burned hers. His hands were cool, but she could feel the brush of his flesh long after he had returned to the bar to pour himself a more-prosaic scotch on the rocks. She sipped the cocktail urgently, glad of the alcohol to strengthen her determination not to be disconcerted by his nearness, but his lean indolence was very appealing, particularly when he pulled off his tie and loosened the top three buttons of his shirt.

'So,' he said, watching her reactions over the rim of his glass, 'shall we sit down?'

Laura subsided on to a low cushioned sofa and tensed anew when he came down beside her, his long legs splayed carelessly across the Chinese carpet. She had never been this close to him before, and the awareness was disturbing. She wanted to remain composed, but it wasn't easy in this position.

'My wife—Regina—has been in Europe for the past six weeks,' he began, suspending his glass between his knees and smoothing its frosted surface with his fingers. 'She's due back day after tomorrow.'

'Yes?' The sound was barely audible, but evidently he heard it and continued:

'Lucia's been with her.'

'Your—daughter.'

'That's right.' He turned his head to look at her, his eyes narrowing. 'Do you like kids, Laura? I guess you do. You're not much more than one yourself, are you?'

'I'm almost twenty-two,' Laura exclaimed defensively, not altogether pleased that he should be thinking of her as a juvenile, however much of a relief it might be in other ways.

'A great age,' he remarked drily. 'Do you realise, I was about your age when Lucia was born.'

'So?' A trace of colour entered Laura's cheeks at the implied impertinence. 'Why do you want to know?'

Jason hesitated. 'Because I have to go to the Big Island at the weekend, and Regina expects me to have charge of Lucia for the next couple of weeks.'

Laura swallowed. 'I still don't—'

'I want you to come to Hawaii with us,' said Jason evenly. 'I need you anyway—in your professional capacity,' he added. 'And I hoped you and Lucia might be company for one another when I'm tied up.'

Laura stared at him helplessly. 'But, I—I—'

'I thought we'd use the yacht,' he went on levelly. 'Kona—that's where we'd be making for—is about a day's sailing from here. It's across the island from Hilo, the capital, but I think you'll enjoy the trip around the coast. We could sail on Friday, spend Saturday on the island, and sail back Sunday. What do you say?'

Laura shook her head. 'I—I've never sailed before.'

'I'm not asking you to take the helm,' he responded wryly. 'I have a crew for that.'

'I might be sea-sick!'

'You might,' he conceded quietly. 'But I don't think you will.'

Laura took another sip of her pina colada. 'Won't your daughter think it odd that I—that I should be coming with you?'

Jason finished his drink and then regarded her sombrely. 'You don't want to come,' he said flatly. 'Why don't you just say so?'

'It's not that,' she burst out quickly, almost before she had considered her words. 'I...I...need time to think.'

'Okay.' Jason got to his feet, a dark shadow over her. 'How much time do you need?'

'I'm not sure.' Laura's shoulders were stiff from the amount of dictation she had taken that day, and almost unconsciously she lifted a hand to massage her aching neck muscles. 'I should have to ask Mrs Sylva.'

'Leave Mrs Sylva to me,' declared Jason crisply, dropping his glass on to an exotically carved map table. 'Here,' he added. 'Let me!' And to her utter distraction, he came round the couch behind her, and pushed her hand away. With expert fingers, he kneaded the throbbing muscles in her shoulders, and then moved to her neck and the slender cords that vibrated beneath his probing touch. 'Better?' he inquired, bending his head to look at her, and it was all she could do not to give in to the almost irresistible urge to rest her head back against his thighs.

'M...much better, thank you,' she murmured, moving

forward out of temptation's way, and with a half smile, he walked across to the bar to pour himself another scotch.

In his absence, Laura finished her drink and got hastily to her feet. She was aware that the upper part of her body was now suffused with colour, and she hated the idea that he might get the wrong impression. But was it the wrong impression? she asked herself impatiently. When Jason had touched her, hadn't she felt as weak and vulnerable as any one of those females who hung on his 'phone at all hours of the day and night? And he probably knew it, she reflected glumly; and was amused by it!

Of course, Laura fell in with his wishes—although it was not entirely due to Jason's persuasion.

Regina Montefiore—she still retained her married name—and her daughter, swept into the office the following morning, having returned from Italy earlier than expected, and both of them stopped short at the sight of Jason's new secretary.

'Where is Marsha?' demanded Regina imperiously, looking round the office as if she suspected the other girl might be hiding from her. 'Who are you? What are you doing here?'

'My name is Laura Huyton and I'm Marsha's temporary replacement,' replied Laura politely, glad Jason had prepared her for this invasion. 'You must be...Mrs Montefiore, and...and Lucia. How do you do? Can I be of some assistance?'

Regina's dark eyes flashed with impatience. It was obvious that, whatever her relationship with her ex-husband, she still resented any change in his staff without her notice. Her colour heightened, and her lips twitched in irritation, and she flicked back her black hair with heavily lacquered nails on fingers fairly dripping with diamonds.

She was certainly very sure of herself, Laura acknowledged tensely, and why not? With voluptuous features, and a body as generously rounded as a Botticelli Venus, she could afford to feel self-confident, and the clothes she wore accentuated her sensual appeal.

Lucia, on the other hand, was more like Jason than Laura had expected. She was dark, but then, so were both her parents, and while Laura could see traces of her mother in the faintly insolent gaze she cast upon the English girl, her height and build were more in keeping with her father's lean frame.

'You can tell Jason I am here,' Regina declared now, tapping impatient fingers on Laura's desk. 'He is here, I suppose. He hasn't disappeared in my absence!'

'He is here, Mrs Montefiore, but he's in a meeting at the moment,' Laura replied carefully. 'He shouldn't be too long. Can I get you and your daughter a cup of coffee while you wait?'

Regina's smile was malicious. 'Just tell him I'm here,' she repeated arrogantly. 'Jason will see me. You'll see.'

Laura's nostrils flared. 'I have orders not to interrupt him, Mrs Montefiore,' she said, controlling her tone with an effort. 'If you and Lucia would like to sit down—'

'Oh, don't be so stupid!' Losing her temper, Regina leant across the desk and pressed down the call button on the intercom. 'Jason!' she said imperiously. 'Will you come and tell this creature who I am!'

There was silence from the other end of the line, but seconds later Jason's door opened and he came out, closing it sharply behind him. Laura dared not look at his face, but Lucia relieved the situation by darting forward and throwing herself against him.

'Daddy!' she exclaimed, wrapping her arms around him. 'Oh, Daddy, I've missed you!'

'Have you, sweetheart?'

Jason's response was more controlled than Laura would have expected, and glancing at Regina she saw the look of satisfaction on her face. If Jason's wife had engineered the whole scene, she could not have chosen a more apt way of defusing the situation, and Laura found herself wondering, rather cynically for her, whether Lucia was used to playing this role.

'I told *her*,' declared Regina contemptuously, flicking a thumb in Laura's direction, 'I told her you would not expect us to wait, Jason, but she would not listen.'

'Miss Huyton has her job to consider,' he responded evenly, releasing himself from Lucia's clinging fingers. 'And you were not supposed to be flying home until tomorrow.'

'So—I got bored!' retorted Regina, the faint accent Laura had noticed deepening as she addressed her ex-husband. 'You are not pleased to see us?' She cast another scornful look in Laura's direction. 'I cannot believe it.'

Jason, too, looked at Laura then, over his daughter's head, and she wondered later if she had only imagined the trace of sympathy that entered his eyes during that brief exchange. 'I'm pleased you arrived back safely, of course,' he replied, transferring his attention back to his ex-wife and leaving Laura with a curiously breathless feeling. 'But I really can't talk to you now. I suggest we have lunch together. Say one o'clock at Bagwells? I'll try not to be late.'

Regina's lips pursed. 'Oh very well. But I came to

warn you—I shall be leaving for New York in the morning. And naturally, I shall expect you to look after Lucy while I'm gone.'

Jason looked down at his daughter. 'Naturally,' he said, a faint smile touching his lips as he met his daughter's somewhat anxious gaze. 'I've already made plans.' He addressed himself to Lucia. 'How does the idea of spending the weekend on the yacht grab you?'

'Oh, Daddy!'

Lucia was evidently excited at the prospect, but Regina's mouth tightened. 'I trust you do not intend to introduce our daughter to your latest mistress, Jason!' she remarked angrily, causing Laura's lips to part in shocked anticipation. 'Or do you really expect me to believe you intend to spend the weekend without female companionship?'

Jason's lean face hardened. 'You can believe what you like, Regina,' he responded dispassionately, and Laura was not the only one to sense the threat inherent in his words.

Regina wavered. 'I just meant—well, I would not have expected you to take Lucy on the yacht without another female in attendance. What if something happens? What if she is sick?'

'Don't worry, Mrs Montefiore.' To her astonishment, Laura realised it was she who had spoken. Getting to her feet, she cast an appealing look at Jason, and then went on, 'I'm going with them, you see. It's partly a business trip.' She paused, aware that Lucia was looking distinctly resentful now. 'I'll look after your daughter, Mrs Montefiore. She'll be quite safe with us.'

CHAPTER SIX

AFTERWARDS, Laura was to feel amazed that she had had the nerve to speak out as she did, but at the time it had seemed the only thing to do. Besides, it did give her a totally unforgivable feeling of satisfaction to beat Regina at her own game, even if Lucia's response was less than enthusiastic.

Still, the die was cast, and on Friday morning Laura was ready when Jason's chauffeur came to pick her up at six o'clock. 'You must be mad!' Sylvie groaned, hearing the other girl moving quietly about the flat before she left, and coming out of her room to speak to her. 'I can't believe you've agreed to spend the weekend on this boat of his. I thought you were the quiet type!'

'Oh, Sylvie! I'm not planning on sleeping with him,' Laura responded hotly. 'His daughter's going with us, you know she is. And he's not interested in me. He's never even made a pass at me.'

'That's what worries me,' retorted Sylvie drily. 'He's played it very cool, I'll give you that. But I hope you're prepared, just in case.'

'Just in case of what?' Laura flushed. 'Oh, Sylvie! Not that again!'

'Why not? D'you want to get pregnant?'

Laura suspected she might need prior notice of that question. The idea of Jason making her pregnant was not one she could consider with equanimity. It was crazy, she knew, and Sylvie would despise her even more if she suspected, but Laura could not avoid the unpalatable fact that emotionally he disturbed her more than any man she had ever known. And the thought of making love with him was something she could not discuss, with anyone.

'Don't be silly,' she said now, stuffing her bikini into her canvas holdall. 'I shall more likely throw up as soon as we get out into the open sea.'

The car came soon after, and Laura drove away feeling far less confident than she appeared. What if Sylvie was right? she fretted. What if Jason did try to make love to her? Her own inexperience had never been a problem before now, but remembering how experienced most of the girls of her acquaintance were, she couldn't help wondering how Jason would react to a twenty-one-year-old virgin!

The sight of the schooner drove all other thoughts from her head—at least temporarily. She had never been aboard such a vessel before, and her absorption in her surroundings helped to ease the situation. It was not easy to treat Jason casually after what Sylvie had said, and in a sleeveless black vest and another pair of the shorts that fit his legs closely to mid-thigh, he was a disturbing presence. Even Lucia's scowling face could not dispel Laura's awareness of him, and she was glad when the anchor was raised and they sailed out of the marina.

Only once in those first few minutes did she forget to be on her guard with him, and that was when she discovered the name of the yacht was the *Laura M.* 'Laura!' she exclaimed, gazing at him with arched brows. 'How did you—'

'It's my mother's name,' he responded softly, his eyes running with disturbing thoroughness over the honey-gold skin of her throat, exposed above the neckline of her sleeveless blouse, and she flushed. 'It was what I wanted to call Lucia, but Regina wouldn't have it. So we compromised. But I still prefer the original.'

Laura looked away from him then, aware of his daughter's sharp eyes watching them. But she couldn't dismiss what he had said as quickly, and her throat dried unpleasantly as she curled her fingers over the rail.

It was a glorious day, albeit a little choppy, once they left the harbour, However, Laura found the pitching motion of the vessel didn't trouble her at all, and seating herself on one of the cushioned loungers, set in the lee of the bulkhead, she turned her face up to the sun.

Lucia was being very unsociable. She had not responded to any of Laura's attempts to make friends with her, and now she was below decks somewhere, taking out her anger on the crew. Laura could hear her complaining voice as she closed her eyes against the glare, and she wondered if the younger girl was really as much like Regina as she seemed.

'Wouldn't you be cooler in something less cumbersome?' suggested Jason quietly, lowering his length on to the chair beside her.

Laura had not heard his approach, and her eyes opened to find her employer regarding her with lazy inquiry. 'I...I burn easily,' she stammered, drawing up her legs and wrapping her arms around her knees. The cotton pants she was wearing were all-enveloping, but the idea of exposing herself before Jason in a bikini was daunting.

'Don't you have any oil?' he asked pointedly, and aware that he could see the bottle of coconut lotion protruding from the bag beside her, she coloured anew.

'Well, yes...'

'Put your swimsuit on,' he recommended flatly. 'I'll see you don't get burned.'

She could have argued, but it seemed pointless. She could hardly spend the whole weekend behaving like an outraged virgin every time he looked at her. Scrambling to her feet, she went down to her cabin and pulled out the skimpy blue bikini.

Back on deck, she discovered Jason had removed his T-shirt and was lying flat out on the cushioned lounger, his closed eyes enabling Laura to reach her own seat without observation. She guessed he would have no problem with over-exposure to the sun. His body was brown and muscular, and already gleaming with moisture, and unable to prevent herself, she allowed her eyes to linger on the arrowing whorls of fine dark hair that disappeared below the waistband of his shorts.

His eyes opened as the chair moved with her weight, and she suffered his appraisal as he reached for the bottle of oil. 'Okay,' he said, sitting up. 'I'll do your back first. Turn over.'

Laura hesitated. 'I can do it...'

'How?' His eyes challenged hers, and she faltered. 'Go on,' he added. 'Lie down. Even I draw the line at performing before an audience.'

Laura rolled on to her stomach. 'I don't know what you mean.'

'I think you do.' He was dispassionate. 'That's what this parade of feminine modesty is all about, isn't it? Someone's told you something about me. Someone's warned you I'm not to be trusted.'

'No!'

'Yes,' he said inflexibly, causing her to gasp in protest when he poured a pool of chilling liquid into the warm hollow of her spine. 'Who was it? Regina? I didn't think you got to know her that well.'

'I didn't.' Laura rested her cheek against her folded arms. 'I hardly spoke to her. You know that.'

'Okay.' He swept the silky curtain of her hair to one side and dipped his fingers into the oil. 'Who then? Luke? Phil Logan?'

'No one,' she persisted, as he began to massage her shoulders. His hands were a forbidden delight, and she couldn't prevent the involuntary surge of pleasure she felt as they moved against her skin. 'Hmm. That feels good.'

'Does it?' With experienced fingers, he released the clip of the bikini bra and stroked the whole sensitive length of her spine to the spot where the band of her briefs rested. 'I'm surprised you let me touch you at all.'

'Mr Montefiore, *please*!' Laura was having difficulty in holding on to her composure. 'I...please, fasten that clip again, will you? I can finish the rest myself.'

Jason ignored her, smoothing ribbons of oil from the curve of her buttocks down over her thighs, and into the sensitive hollow behind her knees. While Laura struggled to attach the two sides of her bikini without lifting her body from the pad, Jason completed his task with evident satisfaction, his fingers probing even the soles of her feet.

When Laura at last scrambled on to her knees, there was a curiously sensuous smile playing around Jason's lips, and she had to force herself to face him without flinching. 'Thank you,' she said, though it was hardly a term of gratitude. 'Can I have the oil now?'

Lucia appeared as Laura finished oiling her midriff, and she looked up at the girl cautiously, prepared to face antagonism of another sort. But to her surprise, Lucia was looking decidedly unhappy, and her pale cheeks and sweating skin told another story.

'Daddy, I don't feel well,' she protested, pressing her hand to her bare stomach. Like her father, Lucia was wearing shorts, with a simple halter top that tied at the back.

Jason came to his feet in a lithe easy movement. 'Don't you, sweetheart?' he murmured, the disturbing gentleness of his smile almost taking Laura's breath away. 'Did you eat anything this morning before we left?'

Lucia shook her head. 'I couldn't. I was too excited,' she mumbled, though Laura had her doubts about that. 'Oh, Daddy! I think I'm going to be sick! Isn't there anything you can do?'

Jason pushed a helpless hand through his hair, and when his eyes encountered Laura's, she put the oil aside and stood up. 'Let me look after her,' she murmured, stepping to Lucia's side and putting a sympathetic arm around the other girl's waist. 'Come on, Lucy. Let's go below.'

Even though Lucia might have preferred to stay with her father, she offered no objections when Laura took her down to her cabin. She was obviously too distressed to put up any real protest, and besides, Laura guessed she was not keen on making a fool of herself in front of Jason. After all, theirs was hardly a normal father-daughter relationship, and Lucia was fast approaching the age when appearances became so important.

In fact, she wasn't sick. After making her comfortable on the bed in her cabin, Laura sped into the forward saloon and purloined a bottle of brandy from the bar. Then, mixing it with a little water, she encouraged the prostrate girl to sip the fiery liquid, hoping that the remedy she had once used on the Channel Islands ferry still held good.

It did. The combination of being flat on her back and the warming glow of the alcohol eventually calmed Lucia's heaving stomach, and a little of the colour returned to her cheeks as she felt the sickness fading.

'Thanks,' she murmured offhandedly, still not prepared to accept Laura unreservedly, and the older girl smiled.

'I should try and sleep, if I were you,' she responded gently, making for the door. 'If you need me, I'll be in my cabin. As it's almost lunchtime, I might as well put my clothes on again.'

'Sorry I spoiled your morning,' Lucia mumbled, turning on to her side away from her, and Laura grimaced.

'No problem,' she said, letting herself out of the door, and Lucia's only response was a sleepy grunt.

She was drying herself after her shower, when she heard someone moving about in her cabin. As she had left her clothes on the bed, she was forced to emerge with only a towel wrapped sarong-wise around her slim body, and she gazed rather apprehensively at her uninvited visitor. Jason was standing gazing broodingly out of the narrow windows that gave the sleeping compartment privacy, his feet slightly apart, his arms folded across the muscled expanse of his chest.

He turned at her appearance, his eyes moving down over her makeshift toga. Then, allowing his arms to fall to his sides, he said quietly, 'I thought for a minute you were sick, too.'

'No. No, I'm fine.' Laura spoke quickly, her nervousness showing. 'Have you seen Lucia? I think she's going to be all right.'

'She's asleep,' said Jason nodding. 'I'm grateful. She and I don't see one another often enough to build a proper relationship.'

Laura hesitated. 'Is that her mother's fault, or yours?'

Jason lifted one dark eyebrow. 'Mine, I guess,' he admitted, although Laura had the suspicion that this wasn't exactly true. Regina might find Lucia an encumbrance sometimes, but she was far too valuable an ally when it came to gaining Jason's attention to be allowed free access to her father.

'Oh, well,' she said now, making a display of securing the towel more closely about her. 'I expect when she's older, she'll be able to choose where she wants to stay.'

Jason did not take her remark the way she had intended. 'What am I to glean from that?' he inquired, tautly. 'That you think Lucia might choose to spend more time with me? You heard what Regina said, my daughter's opinion of her father is not exactly unprejudiced.'

'Even so…'

'Even so, what?'

Laura bent her head. 'It's not really anything to do with me.'

'No, it's not. But I'm interested anyway.' Jason took a step nearer. 'I gather you didn't like Regina.'

'Oh, Mr Montefiore…'

'My name is Jason,' he said flatly. 'Use it. I know all about your English reserve, but in a situation like this, don't you think it's pretty foolish to keep treating me like a stranger.'

'I'm not treating you like a stranger, Mr Montefiore.' Laura licked her dry lips. 'Just as my employer.'

'Your employer, hmm?' Jason's mouth thinned. 'Well, as your employer, I'm asking you to give me your opinion of my ex-wife. Don't you have one?'

Laura sighed. 'Oh, please…'

'Please what?' he snapped, his patience threading.

'For God's sake, Laura, there are times when you make me so angry! What the hell do you expect me to do to you anyway? You've acted like I was going to jump on you ever since you came aboard! Hell, I'm not into forcing myself on anyone—least of all a timid virgin, who doesn't even know what it's all about!'

Laura's face mirrored the pain his cruel words had deliberately evoked, and she automatically fell back a step, her hand pressed to her throat. Sylvie had been *so* wrong, she thought unsteadily, wishing she had not listened to the other girl. She had turned an awkward situation into something worse, and Jason probably assumed she was one of those awful females who thought every man they met couldn't wait to get his hands on them.

'I'm sorry,' he grated now, raking back his hair with obvious frustration, and Laura quickly shook her head.

'It doesn't matter…'

'It does matter,' he retorted harshly, overriding her. 'I didn't mean to say what I did, and I certainly didn't mean it. For Christ's sake, Laura, why do you think I brought you on this trip?'

Laura swallowed a little convulsively. 'You told me.'

'No, I didn't.' Jason turned away from her with an impatient gesture. 'At least, not all of it. I invited you along because I wanted to spend some time with you, away from the office. I like you. You're a nice kid. I guess I never thought it through, that's all.'

Laura absorbed what he was saying with a growing sense of disbelief. 'You mean…'

'I mean I am attracted to you,' he interrupted her flatly. 'And for once in my life, I'm finding it hard to make the running.'

Laura quivered, but she had to say it: 'I—I may be a timid virgin, but I'm not a kid, Jason.'

He half turned to look at her. 'What's that supposed to mean?'

Her courage deserted her. 'I...why...nothing...'

'Laura?' He was in front of her now, his hands descending on her shoulders, his thumbs moving with disturbing sensuality against her flesh. 'Oh hell—look at me!'

She lifted her head reluctantly, half afraid of what he might see in her face, but the smouldering warmth of his irises drove all other considerations out of her head. With a feeling of inevitability, she saw his face descending towards hers, and then his image blurred as his lips found her trembling mouth.

She realised in those first few seconds how often she had wondered what it would be like if Jason kissed her. She had frequently studied his dark face while he was intent on dictation, mentally tracing the taut planes of his features, stroking the silky fringe of his lashes. But she had never expected to find out for herself, or to feel that lean mouth pleasuring hers with so much urgency. The moist flick of his tongue was an added stimulation, and her lips opened wider to allow his hungry invasion.

She gulped for air when he at last released her to bury his face in the silken skein of her hair, and his voice was unsteady as he groped for speech. 'I didn't intend this to happen,' he muttered, one hand beneath her hair caressing the delicate column of her neck. 'At least, not yet anyway,' he added honestly, lifting his head to look down at her. 'Do you mind?'

Laura lifted her hand to touch his cheek, still too bemused by what had happened to be able to think coherently, and with a groan, Jason sought her mouth again.

An uncontrollable surge of pleasure enveloped her when his hands brought her body closer to his, and when next he lifted his head, she murmured in protest.

'You don't know what you're doing,' he said roughly, propelling her gently but firmly away from him. 'Look—I'd better go. Get dressed. We'll have lunch on deck, hmm?'

'Why?' she breathed, still rapt in the emotions he had aroused in her, and with a muffled oath he walked towards the door.

'Because if I don't go now, I won't be able to,' he told her frankly, and her face flamed with colour at the flagrant acknowledgement in his words.

Lucia was able to join them for lunch, and although she ate little of the fresh salmon the chef had prepared, she did enjoy the fruit salad that followed it. If she was aware of any tension between her father and his secretary, she didn't show it, and she even spoke to Laura once or twice, albeit in that same offhand manner she had adopted in her cabin.

For Laura, the meal was something of a trial. She could hardly bear to look at Jason, remembering the abandoned way she had behaved earlier, and she suffered his silent censure of her attire without giving him an opportunity to voice it. But she could not have emerged in a swimsuit again; not after what had happened between them, and although she was overdressed for the occasion, she refused to consider the alternatives.

During the afternoon Jason disappeared into his cabin, apparently to work, and Laura decided to rest. She had hardly slept the night before, and she had been up at five to be ready when Jason's chauffeur appeared. To her surprise, she slept almost immediately, and by the time she woke up, the sun was sinking fast.

Dinner was served in the main saloon. The captain, Alec Cowray, joined them, and Laura was glad she had brought at least one suitable dress. Made of dark blue silk, with a pleated bodice below narrow bootlace straps, the skirt swung flatteringly about her slender legs, and the colour accentuated her extreme fairness and deepened the colour of her eyes.

She was ridiculously pleased when Jason complimented her appearance, and although his comment had been casually made in the presence of his daughter and Alec Cowray, the disruptive quality of his regard over the dinner table could not be ignored.

'Do we have much further to go, Daddy?' Lucia asked, hopefully distracting her father's attention while the waiter re-filled her wine glass, and Jason frowned.

'We'll be lying off the Kona coast by the time you wake in the morning, pretty lady,' Alec Cowray answered gallantly. 'And if you're up at seven you can join me for my early morning dip.'

'I might just do that,' declared Lucia, scowling as her father covered her glass with his hand. 'Will you come, too, Daddy? You don't have any objections to me swallowing too much water, do you?'

'None whatsoever,' responded Jason pleasantly, dark and disturbing in a black shirt and matching pants. Although both men wore ties, jackets had been dispensed with, and Laura didn't blame them. In spite of the trade winds, it was still very warm. 'But I suggest you turn in shortly, if you're planning on matching Alec.'

'And you? Will you come?' Lucia was persistent, and her eyes flickered reluctantly to the other girl. 'And— Laura, too,' she added. 'If she wants.'

'I'd like that,' responded Laura eagerly, glad that Lucia was at least making an effort to be sociable. 'We'll see you at seven, Mr Cowray. All of us.'

'Not me,' said Jason smoothly, putting his napkin aside and getting to his feet. 'Count me out, Alec. Tomorrow's going to be too long a day as it is.'

Laura looked up at him doubtfully, not altogether understanding his explanation, but she averted her eyes when he caught her watching him, and Alec Cowray's departure prevented any further discussion.

Lucia left soon afterwards, the wine she had consumed before her father's embargo causing her eyelids to droop. 'Night, Daddy,' she said, giving him a prolonged hug and a kiss on his cheek, and Jason smiled affectionately as she disappeared out the door.

Left alone with her employer, Laura was tempted to say her good nights too, but Jason forestalled her. 'Let's go up on deck while they clear the cabin,' he suggested quietly, and Laura could think of no reason to refuse.

It was a marvellous night. The sky was inky dark yet, shot with stars, it evoked the image of diamonds on velvet. The powerful schooner seemed to be skimming over the water, its canvas taut against the wind. Laura thought there could be few things more beautiful than a ship under sail, and she shivered with the awareness that she was a part of it.

'You're cold?'

Jason had noticed the involuntary movement, but Laura shook her head. 'Just…exhilarated, that's all,' she murmured, shaking her head in wonder. 'You're very lucky, Jason. This is a beautiful craft.'

'I think so.' Jason relaxed on the rail beside her, his face shadowed in spite of the light from the staterooms. 'I'm glad you feel the same.'

Laura lifted her shoulders. 'Thank you for bringing me.'

Jason hesitated. 'Do you mean that?'

Laura quivered. 'Of course.'

'Even after what happened.'

Laura bent her head. 'Nothing happened.'

'No.' He conceded the point, concentrating on the distant horizon. 'I haven't sunk that low yet.'

'What do you mean?'

'I mean—seducing virgins,' retorted Jason succinctly. 'Shall we talk about something else?'

'Didn't you expect me to be?' asked Laura softly. 'After what you said, I—'

'I hoped you weren't,' replied Jason, turning to face the deck. 'Come on. Let's go and get a drink. I could surely use…'

'Wait!' Laura could not let him go like that. 'Don't you—I mean—is it a crime? Not having had sex, I mean.'

'Don't be foolish!' Jason was impatient.

'Then what is it?' Laura forced him to look at her. 'Am I…am I less desirable because I haven't been with a man before?'

Jason stared at her. 'Do you realise what you're saying?'

Laura flushed. 'Do you?'

Jason made a negative gesture. 'I think the wine has gone to your head.'

'But not to yours.'

'I'm more used to it.' He looked down at her intently for a moment, and then he swore. 'Laura, don't play with fire!'

Laura couldn't help herself. The night; and the yacht; and Jason's disturbing presence—not to mention the

wine she had drunk at dinner—were all combining to
give her a confidence she had never had before, and it
was a tantalising thing, this verbal love-play.

'Why am I playing with fire?' she asked huskily. 'I
asked a perfectly reasonable question.'

'All right, all right.' With a smothered oath, Jason
turned and imprisoned her against the rail between his
hands. 'I'll give you an answer,' he said harshly. '*Yes*!
Yes, you would be more attractive to me if you'd already
slept with another man! Does that satisfy you?'

Laura's bubble burst. 'Thank you,' she mumbled,
barely audibly.

'Don't mention it!' He straightened, releasing her.
'Now shall we go and have that drink?'

'I—I don't think I want one,' said Laura tightly.
'If…if you'll excuse me.'

The door to her cabin had no lock, but in any case,
she didn't need one. Nevertheless, when she lifted her
head from the coverlet some time later to the sound of
someone knocking at her door, she could have wished
for the privacy to shed her tears without interruption.
Had Lucia heard her crying? she wondered, scrubbing
her knuckles across her face. The younger girl's cabin
was just next door. Had her distress been audible even
through the wall?

'Wh…who is it?' she asked in a low voice, hoping
that whoever it was might not hear her and go away, but
there was no reply. Instead, to her horror, the door was
propelled inward, and in the glow from the wall-lights
suspended above the bed, she met Jason's tormented
gaze.

'*Christ*!' he muttered, taking in the situation with one
encompassing look, and leaving the door ajar, he came
across to the bed.

He was wearing a dark red kimono-style robe, embroidered around the hem and cuffs, and she guessed from his bare legs below its folds that it was all he was wearing. His hair was damp, as if he had just taken a shower, and she could smell the tangy fragrance of some lotion he had been using.

'I thought it must be you,' he said, looking down at her with brooding eyes, and then, startling her by his strength, he bent down and lifted her up into his arms. 'We can't talk here,' he added, when she gave him a tearful glance, and without giving her time to protest, he strode back to the door.

Jason's suite was infinitely more masculine in design, his bed, where he eventually deposited her, strewn with dark brown silk sheets, and a figured brown and gold bedspread. He had evidently been reading—there was a file tossed carelessly on to the table beside the bed and the distinctive aroma of brandy indicated he had been having a nightcap.

Leaving her for a moment, he went into his sitting room to fetch her a glass, and presently he pressed a goblet of the same remedy she had given Lucia earlier in the day into her hand. 'Drink it,' he said, sitting down beside her in a partly cross-legged position. 'It won't make you drunk, but it might make you sleep.'

Laura sniffed. 'I'm sorry.'

'Why are you sorry?'

'For…for making a fool of myself. I don't…usually.'

Jason's mouth took on a sardonic slant. 'I should hope not.'

'No. I mean it.' Laura took a sip of the brandy and grimaced. 'What must you think of me?'

Jason regarded her with some irony. 'I think you know.'

'No, I don't.' She sniffed again, and he handed her a box of tissues. 'Oh, this is so embarrassing!'

Jason waited until she had composed herself, and then he said softly, 'Do you want to stay?'

Laura's lips parted. 'You mean—here?'

Jason took the glass that was in danger of spilling itself all over the sheets out of her hand. 'Where else?'

Laura gazed at him. 'You mean—sleep with you?'

'I mean—sleep with me,' he conceded. 'God knows, it's what I want!'

'But...you said...'

'I lied,' he admitted huskily, taking her wrist to his lips and caressing the sensitive inner curve with his tongue. 'Laura, I'm about ten years older than you are. And I know there are plenty of people more than willing to tell you the kind of guy they think I am. We both know what I *should* do, and that's why I said what I did.'

'Jason—'

'No, listen!' He bent his head and silenced her with his mouth. 'If you stay, you know what will happen. I'm a man, not a saint. I don't admire myself for this, but I know what I'm doing. Just be sure you do, too.'

It was not until she was in Honolulu that Laura really considered what Jason had said, and by then it was much too late to have second thoughts. Still, she did take Sylvie's advice about birth control. She had no wish to present Jason with the news that he had fathered another child, and although the idea of having his baby was one she cherished, she was practical enough to realise that that was not her role.

Fathoms deep in love with him, though she was, she knew he had never once said he loved her. He wanted her; she had no doubt about that. Indeed, within two weeks of their becoming lovers, he had asked her to move into his apartment with him, and although Laura had hung out for a further four weeks, eventually she had succumbed to his expert persuasion.

Besides, she had wanted to be with him equally as much as he wanted to be with her. Getting up and dressing, and allowing him to drive her back to the lonely isolation of her own bed in the early hours of the morning soon lost its appeal, and it was a tantalising delight to wake in the mornings and find him beside her. To feel his lean, muscular frame wrapped possessively about her was a very satisfying experience, and she also came to appreciate the other advantages that came from being there when he woke.

Nevertheless, she had no illusions that one day Jason would find someone else. He was not the kind of man to be content with the same woman for too long, and Regina was always about to maliciously remind Laura— as if she could ever forget—that she was only the latest in a long line of females.

'It isn't as if you're anything special,' she remarked, on one occasion, her lips tilting scornfully. 'I mean, I understood Jason's desire to wipe that smug touch-me-not expression off your face, but even I couldn't hold him after Lucy was born. And you have to admit, I have a little more to do it with than you have!'

Laura had weathered these comments manfully, and their association continued even after his secretary, Marsha, returned to her desk. Indeed, Jason took advantage of the fact, encouraging Laura to give in her notice at the agency so that he could take her with him on his frequent trips to the mainland. He even introduced her to his sister and his mother, though his relations with his father were rather less cordial. Laura knew it had something to do with Marco Montefiore's business dealings, but she didn't probe. If Jason wanted her to know, he would tell her. She believed they had few secrets from one another.

Two years into their relationship, she was actually beginning to feel her position was secure, and that was why, when the bombshell exploded, she was so unprepared to deal with it. Discovering Jason had been deceiving her was bad enough; discovering he was also responsible for another man's death was intolerable.

She had tried to discuss it with him. She had tried to tell him how she felt, and how he had hurt her, but he wouldn't listen. In one terrible afternoon, her whole world had been shattered, and she had never thought she would pick up the pieces again...

CHAPTER SEVEN

THE WARM WATERS of the Pacific were distinctly clearer now as the Learjet began its descent towards the island. For hours they had been flying west and south over a blue expanse of ocean that was totally indistinguishable from more than thirty thousand feet. But now, having glimpsed landfall over Molokai, they were rapidly losing height in their approach to Kaulanai, and in spite of her misgivings, Laura could not deny a certain sense of anticipation.

It was perfectly natural, she told herself firmly, when an inner voice chided her weakness. Whether she liked it or not, the island was to be her home until Pamela had had the baby, and she could hardly be blamed if she was curious to see the house Jason had built.

The fact that Pamela was already there had come as something of a shock. When Laura had left San Francisco, the arrangement had been that she should return there after settling her own affairs in London, thus giving her sister time to dispose of the apartment she had been leasing, and pack her belongings ready for the transfer to Kaulanai. But instead, Jason had gone to see Pamela in her absence, and offered the services of his lawyer to facilitate matters for her. And her sister, much to Laura's astonishment, had accepted his offer, and in consequence Pamela had been living in Jason's house for the past three days, enjoying the freedom of a total lack of responsibility. That was why he had flown to London, Jason had explained, in the drowsy aftermath of his lovemaking. Not to spy on her, but to inform her of the change in arrangements, which meant she had no reason to land on the mainland, after all.

To say that Laura had been taken aback by this new development was an understatement. She had believed Pamela's acceptance of Jason's suggestion had been apathetic at best, and she had been half prepared to face an argument on her return. In spite of the obvious advantages of his offer, she had been surprised that her sister had apparently given up her search for Mike Kazantis. For although Laura had made some vague reference to the fact that Jason had promised to inquire into his whereabouts, she had told Pamela nothing of his relationship with Jason. She had not even told her he was married, which she could have done quite easily. To say that Jason knew of him and not to elaborate on it, had made her feel quite a fraud. But until Pamela had been satisfactorily installed on Kaulanai, she had not wanted to say anything to upset her, and it had been somewhat troubling to discover that Pamela's state of mind had not been as emotionally fragile as she had thought.

'Are you tired?'

Jason's controlled inquiry above her brought her head up with a start, and she was annoyed to feel the blood surging into her face. If he could be so objective about it, why couldn't she? she asked herself fiercely, despising her reactions to his hard muscled body. It was incredibly difficult for her to put what had happened the night before out of her mind, but although he had been left in no doubt as to her contempt for his behaviour, he showed a cool indifference to her feelings. The heated accusations she had flung at him in the sobering light of morning had left him cold, and getting up he had put on his clothes and left her, without so much as a word of apology. He had evidently no regrets for what had happened, and she loathed herself utterly for making it so easy for him. By making love to her, he had successfully re-established his claim to her body, and no matter what happened subsequently, he had proved his superiority over her.

'A little,' she mumbled now, in answer to his question, conscious that the young stewardess, Julie, was close enough to overhear their conversation. It had been a long journey, and although the afternoon sun was still shining on the islands, her metabolism was telling her it was already the early hours of the next morning.

'Did you sleep?' Jason persisted, and she was forced to look up at him once again. In black Levi's and a matching cotton shirt, the sleeves rolled back to his elbows, exposing the fine hairs covering his forearms, he looked disruptively handsome, and Laura ducked her head swiftly to evade his probing appraisal. It was unfair, she thought, that even the slight pouches beneath his eyes, evidence of the exhausting night he had spent, only added to his dark magnetism. His raw masculinity was as natural to him as the sexuality he exuded without effort. He was aware of it, she was sure of that, and he would use it if he had to, but she was determined he would never know the effect it had on her.

'A little,' she murmured, linking her fingers together in her lap. 'Did you?'

It was a perfunctory inquiry, made for Julie's benefit, but he chose to answer it, squatting down beside her with lazy indolence. 'For a while,' he conceded softly, running long fingers over the arm of her chair, so that she had to press her arm to her side to avoid his touch. 'I rested on the bed for a while,' he added, and the emotion in his voice was unmistakable now. 'I thought you might have joined me...'

Laura quivered. 'You didn't think any such thing!'

'Why not?' His voice was still deceptively soft, but there was a faint edge which had not been there before. 'There's nothing new about us sharing a bed—'

'*Stop it*!' Laura cast an imploring glance in Julie's direction, but the stewardess had disappeared into the forward cabin to speak to the pilot and they were completely alone. 'Why must you torment me? Do you get some perverted kind of enjoyment out of it?'

'Was I tormenting you?' Abruptly, he straightened. 'How am I supposed to take that? You didn't exactly claw my eyes out last night, did you? Although, I have to say, I have several weals in other places, which seems to prove something.'

'Jason, *please*!'

'I disgust you, I know. You said this morning.' His lips twisted. 'Unfortunately, that's something *you're* going to have to live with.'

He left her then, crossing the cabin of the plane to fling himself into an armchair at the opposite side, and Laura fumbled awkwardly for her seat belt as the powerful little jet came down low over the ocean. The island was just ahead of them now, the creaming swirl of water marking the reef giving way to turquoise shallows lapping on sand bleached almost white by the sun. It was breathtakingly lovely, truly an island paradise, accorded Laura reluctantly, and she would not have been human if she had not felt a surge of wonder at its beauty.

The thin blade of the runway appeared beyond a belt of tall pandanus palms, whose roots were bedded in a thicket of shrubs and flowering plants. The ribbon of tarmac shimmered in a haze of heat, looking scarcely long enough to accommodate the plane. But the Learjet landed smoothly, the screaming reverse-thrust of its engines bringing it quickly to a halt. As it did so, a fluttering flock of doves rose protestingly from the bushes, scattering scarlet petals in the headlong panic of their flight.

As soon as the plane had landed, Jason flicked open his safety belt and got to his feet, gathering together the few belongings he had brought with him on the flight The black suede jacket he had needed at Heathrow, he now slung carelessly over one shoulder, and the briefcase, whose contents he had studied during the early part of the trip, was closed and locked securely before it was suspended from his hand.

Realising he was waiting for her to make a move, Laura unfastened her own seat belt and stood up as Frank Danielli came through from the forward cabin. 'Good flight, Frank,' said Jason evenly, never forgetting to treat his employees with respect, and the older man smiled.

'Just a little turbulence over northern Canada,' he admitted ruefully, flexing his shoulder muscles with weary satisfaction. 'I don't mind telling you, Jase, I'm looking forward to a hot soak and a cold beer! Just don't ask me to fly back to London again in the foreseeable future! That's some trip, and Clark and I have made it four times in the last seven days!'

'Request granted,' said Jason, with an easy grin, and Laura's stomach tightened at his casual charm. Despite his attraction for the opposite sex, he was equally relaxed in male company, and she didn't need to see Frank Danielli's responding grin or hear Clark Sinclair's chuckle of laughter to know that here were two more people who regarded him with affection.

The door of the jet was unlocked, and thrusting it outwards, Clark uncoiled the flight of steps concealed in its structure. 'Home sweet home,' he remarked, stepping back to allow Jason to precede him down on to the tarmac, and Laura realised there was no element of censure in the friendly glance he cast in her direction.

Following Jason down the steps, she was glad now she had not succumbed to the urge to wear the jersey suit she had first put on that morning. In the chill of Jason's departure, she had felt the need for something warmer than the cotton shirt and pants she had planned to wear. But sanity had prevailed, and now, stepping out into the heat of an Hawaiian afternoon, she applauded her choice.

After bidding goodbye to the crew, Jason nodded towards a cream convertible parked at the edge of the runway. 'Let's go,' he said, his tone cooling perceptibly when he spoke to her, and Laura cast a doubtful glance over her shoulder.

'My cases,' she murmured, wondering if he had forgotten, but Jason merely gestured her onward.

'Frank will see they're sent on,' he declared, nodding a greeting to an olive-skinned Chinese boy, dressed in beige overalls, who was already sprinting towards the plane. 'Don't worry. You won't have to sleep in the raw—not unless you want to, of course.'

Laura pressed her lips tightly together. 'Must you keep making remarks like that?' she asked, curiously near to tears, and his expression softened slightly.

'Must you keep pretending you didn't want me just as much as I wanted you?' he countered harshly, and she turned her head away.

'You forced me...'

'Only up to a point,' retorted Jason curtly. 'I've never raped a woman in my life!'

'I never said you raped me—'

'You damn near implied it,' he returned, reaching the car and tossing his briefcase carelessly into the back. Then, recovering his expression, he turned to give the young man leaning on the car a friendly smile. 'Hi, Jonah,' he greeted him cheerfully, giving Laura another demonstration of his rare ability to adapt himself to any situation. 'How's your mother? Did she take those tablets Luke sent her?'

'Yes, sir, Mr Montefiore,' exclaimed Jonah self-importantly, swinging open the passenger door for Laura to get inside, and as she did so, the name Jason had used made her briefly forget their antagonism.

'Luke, Jason?' she probed, as he fitted his length behind the driving wheel. 'Do you mean Lucas Kamala?'

'So you do remember some things,' remarked Jason drily, and Laura guessed she deserved his cynicism.

'I remember Luke,' she declared defensively, as Jonah vaulted into the back of the vehicle. How could she forget the charming Hawaiian who had first made her welcome at the club? He had always been so kind to her, and she had missed his gentle humour more than she realised. 'Where is he now?'

'Where he always was,' replied Jason, casting a reflective glance in her direction before flicking the ignition. 'At the Blue Orchid. He's in charge there now.' He paused. 'You should have asked for him. He might not have told me of your call.'

Laura frowned. 'What do you mean?'

'Luke cares about me,' responded Jason obliquely, setting the car in motion, and before she could ask him what he meant, he started to speak to Jonah again.

But his words gave her something to think about as the road from the airstrip wound upwards, through a glade of pine and eucalyptus trees, to emerge on a gravelled track some distance above the shoreline. From above, it was possible to see the shape of the beach as it wound around a jutting headland. It was also possible to see cultivated fields stretching away from the coast, fields planted with banana and pineapple, and the waving stalks of sugar cane. Laura gazed about her in wonder, realising as she did so that the island she had assumed accommodated only Jason's house and its surroundings was really a thriving community.

The village, when they reached it, proved her theory, with a cluster of cottages set about a square, with a general stores and petrol pumps to service its inhabitants. A stream ran through the middle of the village, and there was a shaky wooden structure spanning it, which scarcely looked strong enough to support the powerful car. But Jason negotiated it easily, waving to the group of children who ran to shout a greeting. The mix of Chinese and Polynesian blood was reflected in their faces, and Laura was forcibly reminded of the beauty in these islands. The older girls regarded Jason with open admiration, and looking at their sweep of ebony hair and the dusky symmetry of their features, she couldn't help wondering what he could see in her unremarkable appearance. Compared to their vivid warmth and colour, she felt pale and uninteresting. She could only believe that what he had said just two weeks ago was true. He did resent her defiance in walking out on him, and he was determined to make her pay for it, one way or the other.

'Is Miss Pamela all right?' Jason asked Jonah suddenly, and Laura put her own anxieties aside to turn and look at the young man behind them. Apart from Jason's casual explanation, in the somnolent afterglow of his lovemaking, they had not discussed her sister's condition at all, and the bitter acrimony of his leave-taking had created a barrier between them that had made further communication impossible. But now, he had made a direct reference to Pamela's presence in his house, and Laura waited in anticipation for Jonah's reply.

'She's fine,' he responded swiftly. 'Leah's looking after her real well.'

'Leah!' echoed Laura disbelievingly, and Jason pulled a wry face.

'Another blast from the past?' he inquired mockingly. 'You didn't think I'd lose a good housekeeper like Leah, did you? She's been with me for too many years to leave now.'

Laura shook her head. 'I never thought she'd leave Oahu.'

'I didn't either,' admitted Jason, with a shrug. 'But I guess I mean more to her than we thought. Strange, isn't it? I'd have gambled my soul she was more likely to walk out on me than…anyone else.'

Laura rested her elbow on the door, her fingers plucking nervously at the glossy paintwork. 'But, you did, didn't you?' she murmured huskily. 'Gamble your soul, I mean. There's more than one way to risk immortality.'

'Now, who's making nasty remarks?' he demanded in an undertone, using the accelerator to mask his words, and she expelled the air in her lungs on an unsteady breath.

Forcing herself to concentrate on her surroundings instead of on the disturbing presence of the man beside her, Laura shaded her eyes against the glare of the lowering sun. The narrow road had descended almost to sea level again, and the brilliance of the sun-streaked water was blinding. But she couldn't be absolutely sure the moistness of her eyes was only the result of physical causes. There was a tightness in her chest that had nothing to do with the beauty of the island, and she wondered how Jason could hurt her so easily when she hated him so much.

Minutes later, the perplexities of her emotions were forgotten as they turned between the white gateposts which marked the boundary of Jason's house. A narrow paved drive curved around a bank of flowering hibiscus, and then mounted a gentle incline to where flame trees framed a sprawling plantation-style house. White painted with louvred green shutters folded back beside all the windows, it had a wide terrace flanked with tall columns, that supported the iron-railed balcony above. Shallow steps flowed along the front façade, blending into stone urns, overflowing with creamy camellias and scarlet poinsettias. The terrace curved gracefully round the sides of the house, where clipped green lawns sloped towards a cluster of papayas. The back evidently faced the ocean. Laura could hear its muted thunder as she got herself out of the car. The house had evidently been built to take advantage of the trades, and she guessed they would keep it deliciously cool, even on the hottest day.

'It's…beautiful,' she murmured, her hand lingering on the car door as she looked up at its simple elegance, and Jason gave her a considering look.

'Then you won't find living here such a hardship, will you?' he observed, sliding out of the car to stand beside her.

Her breath caught in her throat before she asked quickly: 'Where's Pam?'

The emergence of an enormously fat Polynesian

woman from the house prevented his reply, and Laura waited a little nervously when Jason went to meet her. After the way Phil Logan had behaved, and Jason's own reactions to her return, she was not at all convinced that his housekeeper would make her welcome, and although she told herself it hardly mattered, she was apprehensive just the same.

'Have you really been to London and back again, Jason?' the woman exclaimed, enfolding him in her ample embrace. Her dark eyes closed briefly, as if to say a prayer of thanks for his safe return, and then opened to encompass Laura's anxious face. 'You're looking tired,' she added, drawing back to study his lean features. 'You had any sleep at all since you left?'

'Enough.' Jason's tone was tolerant, but he turned to include Laura in their exchange. 'You see, Leah,' he said, 'I brought her back, like I promised. You'd better tell her you're pleased to see her. I think she's afraid you're going to break her legs.'

'I am not.' Laura's lips tightened, and her blue eyes flashed her indignation in the moments before Leah came between them. 'It's good to see you again, Leah. I hope you don't object to this invasion.'

'It's Jason's house. I'm only his housekeeper, missy,' Leah declared, giving the girl the same comprehensive appraisal she had given her employer. 'It's been a long time. You fixing on staying this time?'

Laura hesitated. 'If you'll have me,' she murmured, her eyes meeting Leah's dark ones with steady determination, and the housekeeper glanced at Jason over her shoulder.

'She's grown up,' she remarked, returning her gaze to Laura and revealing a reluctant admiration. And although Laura didn't care for their deliberate provocation, she controlled the impulse to voice it, and won Leah's tacit approval.

'Where's Pamela?' she asked again, feeling that was safer ground, and Leah arched her dark brows.

'She'll be over later, I guess,' she replied, somewhat obscurely, and Laura lifted her eyes to Jason's dark face.

'Over?' she echoed, the one word epitomizing her lack of comprehension, and with an impatient look at the housekeeper, he said:

'She's here. Don't worry. I guess she's resting right now. Yes?' This, as Leah's chins wobbled her assent. 'Okay. I suggest you go and freshen up. Leah will show you your room. Then, later on, we'll all have a drink together.'

Laura wanted to ask exactly where Pamela was, and why she couldn't simply go to *her* room instead, but she did feel hot and sticky, and the idea of freshening up was appealing.

'All right,' she said, unable to penetrate the cool mask of his expression, and with a helpless shrug of her shoulders, she followed Leah into the house.

Half an hour later, she stepped through french doors on to the balcony opening off the bedroom behind her. From the moment Leah had shown her into these apartments, she had been conscious of the fantastic view, and although washing her face and hands, and sluicing the moist area beneath her breasts had taken more time than she had anticipated, she could not resist this fleeting glimpse of what lay beyond the windows.

As she had thought, the back of the house faced the ocean just far enough away to allow for a stone-tiled patio and the sickle curve of a swimming pool. Beyond the thatched cabanas, used for changing, soft dunes

sloped down to a beach washed clean by the incoming
tide. Between nubby-trunked palms, the Pacific creamed
on damp sand, unmarred by any human footprint—blue-
green waters shedding skeins of foam over grains of
coral. It was a scene out of a city-dweller's imagination;
a desert island, complete with tropic seas and waving
palms.

But then, the house too, had all the attributes of a
dream home. From the moment Laura had stepped on to
the cool marquetry of the terracotta-tiled floor, she had
been aware of its style and elegance, an impression re-
inforced as Leah took her up the fan-shaped staircase
with its ivory banister rail.

There were paintings everywhere, large and small,
grouped and singly hung, upon walls colour-washed for
coolness. A sunburst of a chandelier was suspended from
the arching roof of the atrium-styled entrance hall, which
in its turn created a natural gallery, around which all the
upper rooms were spaced.

Laura had no doubt that the rooms into which she was
shown comprised the master suite. A generous sitting
room, furnished in shades of cream and gold, possessed
a buttoned sofa and a matching armchair in rich ivory
velvet. There were polished oriental cabinets, and a
screen of evidently Japanese origin, all set on a dusty-
gold carpet, whose design was cleverly muted.

The bedroom opening from it was equally as large,
though the bed that occupied less than half the space
was what imprisoned Laura's gaze. Like the room itself,
it was huge, and although the headboard was conserva-
tively carved the coverlet thrown upon it was a vivid
splash of jade.

'I'll leave you to wash and freshen up,' said Leah,
after assuring herself that the girl was suitably im-

pressed, and Laura was left to explore the imposing bathroom away from the housekeeper's watchful gaze. Nevertheless, she had still been somewhat daunted by the two circular step-in tubs, with their added sophistication of jacuzzi attachments. Smoked glass threw back her reflection from a dozen different angles, and she suspected one would have to have a fine conceit not to find something of dissatisfaction in so many refractions of one's personality.

Now, as she rested her hands on the cool wrought-iron that fenced the balcony, she found herself wondering how many of Jason's women had used that bathroom with him, and her stomach contracted. It was all very well for Leah to treat her with a mixture of disapproval and speculation, but how had she reacted to the women who had taken Laura's place?

Her thoughts were so distasteful to her, the view no longer had the power to hold her interest, and abandoning both she found her way out of the apartments. The house was quiet as she descended the stairs, and she paused for a moment in the impressive entrance hall, trying to get her bearings. To her right, a scalloped row of arches gave on to elegant withdrawing rooms and Laura was briefly struck by the contrast evoked by dark green alcoves set in stark white walls. But although she was tempted to explore these rooms, which might reveal yet another facet of Jason's character, she turned in the direction she hoped would lead to the back of the house. A sun-lit corridor promised success, and after a few moments she emerged into the sun-baked heat of the patio.

To her surprise, there was no one about, though the striped cushioned loungers by the pool looked inviting. The blue-tiled pool looked inviting, too, but she was too exhausted at present to contemplate its pleasures. Maybe

tomorrow, she thought, her pulse quickening at the unwilling realisation that she was actually here, in Jason's
house; that she was *committed*. It was an unreal sensa-
tion, made the more so by the distinct feeling of jet-lag
that was gripping her. It didn't seem possible that less
than twenty-four hours ago she had been in London, and
despite the proof in front of her, the whole situation was
acquiring the vague insubstantiality of a dream.

She swayed a little, putting a hand to her head, and
started when a hard masculine arm came around her.
'You're worn out,' Jason murmured softly, his tone almost gentle, but she pulled herself away to face him.

'What you mean is—I look a hag!' she exclaimed,
tears not far from the surface. 'Wh...where is Pam?'

'Here she is now,' he responded flatly, and leaving
her he went to meet the tawny-haired young woman who
was just crossing the lawns towards them. Cool and dismissive, he ignored her look of surprise, and Laura expelled a shaky, confused breath before going after him.

'You're back!' Pamela's greeting was relaxed and
welcoming, and Laura had to squash the unworthy
thought that for someone who was just getting over an
attempted suicide, her sister looked healthier than she
had ever seen her. She accepted Laura's kiss and smiled.
'Isn't this a heavenly place?'

'Heavenly,' agreed Laura, hoping her sister would not
notice the edge in her voice. 'How are you, Pam? Where
were you?'

'Oh, didn't Jason tell you?' Pamela turned easily to
the man beside her. 'I'm staying in the bungalow—over
there.' She waved her hand carelessly towards the trees.
'Jason thought it would be easier for me than staying in
the main house. I've got my own maid and my own
kitchen, and I can be quite self-sufficient if I choose to

be.' She touched Jason's arm with evident affection. 'Of course, I haven't up till now. Before he went away, Jason and I ate together, didn't we?'

'We did.'

Jason returned her smile, and Laura felt her stomach clench with painful emotion. 'How nice,' she murmured, unable to avoid the fact of their easy cordiality, and although she knew she was tense and over-tired, it suddenly seemed the last straw.

'Well,' she said, as they walked back to the patio together, 'I don't suppose you'd mind if I left you to yourselves this evening.' She ignored Jason's sudden intake of breath, and continued raggedly, 'I am very tired. I suppose the journey—so many miles…the time change—' She broke off unsteadily, and forced a faint smile. 'I'm sorry, Pam, but I don't think I can keep my eyes open any longer.'

A maid was unpacking her suitcases in the bedroom when Laura reached the sitting room of the suite, but she hardly registered the fact of their arrival.

'Please,' she said, realising she was going to cry and unable to do anything about it, 'I can finish these. Just—just leave them, won't you? I don't need any further assistance.'

The young maid, who had been hanging her clothes away in the closets of the dressing room that lay between the bedroom and the bathroom, looked doubtful. 'But Leah said—'

'I'll speak to Leah,' cut in Jason's harsh tones, and the girl flushed. 'You can finish in the morning,' he added, pointedly holding the door open, and with a little bob of her head, the maid left them.

Alone with him, Laura took a deep breath. Coping with the maid had strained her resources to their limit, but coping with Jason was something else entirely. Without waiting for the censure, which she was sure was why he had followed her, she dived into the bathroom, only to gaze about her in dismay when she discovered there was no lock on the door. Her paltry weight was easily propelled away by Jason's forced entry, and he stood looking at her distractedly as she wrapped her arms about her.

'What in hell do you think you're doing?' he demanded. He shook his head. 'I thought you were all-fire keen to see your sister.'

'I was. I—I am.' Laura shivered. 'I'm sorry.'

'Like hell!' Jason raked back his hair with an impatient hand. And then, as if acknowledging her complete exhaustion, he swore rather more colourfully. 'Okay, okay,' he said tersely. 'You win. Get undressed and get into bed. This is going to look a whole lot different in the morning.'

'Do you think so?' Laura's throat ached with the effort of keeping her tears at bay, and as if sensing the extent of her imbalance, Jason hauled her not ungently towards him.

'Believe it!' he told her harshly, running his hands along the curve of her neck. 'Do you want me to undress you?'

Laura jerked back as if he had struck her. 'As you did last night?' she choked, and with a twisted snarl, Jason turned away.

'You have to be kidding!' he grated brutally, his eyes raking her with unconcealed contempt. 'You're right,' he added. 'You do look a hag! And I don't happen to be that desperate!'

CHAPTER EIGHT

LAURA AWAKENED to the scent of roses and verbena, the distinctive perfumes of a dozen different blossoms mingling with the salty tang of the sea, and drifting irresistibly in through the open shutters.

Turning her head on the fine linen pillowcase, she saw the open balcony doors and frowned. She could have sworn she had closed them before going to bed, but her memory of the night before was so hazy, she could have been mistaken. She blinked, stretching luxuriously beneath the thin sheet, which was all that covered her, and then gathered her knees up tight against her chest as a spasm of apprehension swept over her. Where was Jason? Twisting her head still further, she waited for her eyes to alight on the other occupant of the bed, but to her surprise—and relief—she was alone.

Turning over fully, she realised the place beside her had not even been slept in, and her brows, several shades darker than her hair, drew together in unwilling comprehension. Jason had not shared her bed. Wherever he had slept, it had not been beneath the sheets of this colonial-styled four poster, and remembering her opinion that these were the principal apartments of the house, she wondered rather anxiously where he had laid his head.

Propping herself up on one elbow, she ran a thoughtful hand over her untidy braid of hair. Dipping down to her breasts, it drew attention to the fact that the strap of her nightgown had slipped off one shoulder, and she pulled it up absently as she gazed across the room with troubled eyes.

What time was it? she wondered, twisting her watch round on her wrist so that she could see its face. Five o'clock, she read, without enthusiasm. The sun was so bright, she had thought it was much later.

Sighing, she slumped back against the pillows, not wanting to remember her behaviour of the night before, but incapable of avoiding it as her brain cleared. She had behaved childishly, she knew, running out on Pamela, as if her sister was to blame for her predicament. But she had felt so strange and disorientated, and Pamela's apparent acceptance of the situation had seemed like a betrayal.

Shaking her head, she put up a slightly unsteady hand and began to loosen the woven strands of her hair. Perhaps, after a shower, she would feel less conscious of her own shortcomings, she thought flatly. Right now, she was far too aware of Jason's savage condemnation, and his brutal words were still resounding in her head.

The incisive sound of something—or someone—slicing into the pool below her windows brought her foot tentatively out of bed. There was a distinct difference between the surging roar of the ocean and the crisp lap of water on tiles, and swiftly crossing the floor, she ventured out on to the balcony.

The warmth of the sun was revitalising, the strengthening rays still containing an element of coolness that dispelled the sense of lethargy still gripping her. Breathing deeply, hardly aware that with her hair loose about her shoulders she looked bemused and slightly fey-like, she leaned her arms on the balcony rail, and gazed down at the dark head in the pool.

It was Jason. There was no mistaking the lithe muscularity of his body cleaving through the water, leaving a rippling backwash in its wake. He was covering the pool easily, his vigorous strokes taking him swiftly from one end to the other. At each turn, he performed an underwater somersault to head him back in the opposite direction, and Laura's attention was briefly held by the speed of this manoeuvre.

But her initial instincts were to draw back and leave him to his solitary enjoyment. She had no wish to be observed. Yet, she assured herself, it was much too early for him to expect her to be about, and there was something rather pleasurable about watching him, unseen.

Her innocent voyeurism was rudely arrested when he swam to the side of the pool, and pulled himself out of the water. He was naked, the powerful muscles of his body exposed as he swept the excess moisture out of his hair with a careless hand and bent to pick up the towel lying on a chair nearby. Rubbing himself dry, he was unconsciously sensual in his movements, and in spite of everything that had gone before, Laura could not deny the unwilling stimulation of her senses.

Then, as if sensing her eyes upon him, he looked up, and Laura had no chance to avoid his gaze, even if she had wanted to. Besides, to dart back into the room would have been an admission of guilt, and she had nothing to feel guilty of, she told herself fiercely.

'Did you sleep well?' he inquired, dropping the towel to pick up a dark red towelling robe, and Laura pretended to look at the distant ocean as he tied the cord about his waist.

'I slept very well, thank you,' she replied tensely. It was nothing less than the truth, and she felt infinitely rested this morning. 'Did you?'

'Do you care?' he countered, tipping back his head to

look at her, and she acknowledged that his cynicism was not entirely misplaced.

'You're up very early,' she ventured, changing the subject and he shrugged.

'It's almost half-past-seven,' he responded. 'I suppose it depends what you call early. I often get up at this hour.' He paused. 'Particularly if I'm sleeping alone.'

The content of his words overwhelmed her instinctive embarrassment, and she frowned. 'Half-past seven?' she echoed. 'I only make it half-past five!'

'That's because your watch is still set for London time,' essayed Jason flatly. 'You've slept for the best part of fifteen hours. Come down, and we'll have breakfast together.'

Laura hesitated. 'I was going to take a shower.'

'Take it later.' Jason regarded her steadily. 'Come as you are. You can always take a dip in the pool.'

Laura swallowed. 'All right.' She moistened her lips. 'Give me five minutes.'

'You got it,' he responded laconically, with a lazy inclination of his head, and Laura hurried back inside, her heart beating rather quickly.

The dressing room was a shambles. The maid had managed to hang most of her crushable clothes away the night before, but her half-empty suitcases were still lying on the floor, strewn with filmy underwear and shoes still wrapped in tissue paper. She had found the cotton nightdress she was wearing and left everything else, and now she made another invasion, rummaging about for a swim suit.

She rinsed her face at one of the twin hand-basins that lined the opposite wall of the dressing room from the long fitted closets. Above the basins, a bank of mirrors had little compassion for her pale complexion, but her skin was good and she hadn't the time—or the inclination—to use cosmetics. She hesitated longest over her hair, half convinced she should restore it to its usual neatness, but time was pressing, and it did protect her shoulders from the sun. On impulse, she simply ran a brush through it, and snatching up a thigh-length beach wrap and dark glasses, she left the room.

It was not until she was halfway down the stairs that she realised how submissively she had rushed to do Jason's bidding, and deliberately slowing her footsteps, she tried to govern her racing pulses. But it was useless; she had no control over her emotions, and giving up the effort, she allowed a trembling breath to escape her.

By the time she emerged into the sunshine, a glass-topped table had been set beneath a circular umbrella, with a jug of freshly-squeezed orange juice looking infinitely inviting to Laura's thirsty eyes. A coffee pot was giving off the rich aroma of ground beans, and warm rolls filmed the perspex cover of a serving dish.

'I took the liberty of ordering for both of us,' remarked Jason appearing from the direction of the cabanas, and Laura's lips parted at the sight of his lean bronzed body. He had shed the towelling robe in favour of frayed denim shorts, and his almost animal magnetism was distinctly pronounced.

'Thank you.'

Glad of the protection of her sun glasses, Laura slipped into a bamboo-framed chair at the table, and helped herself to some orange juice.

'Aren't you warm with that thing on?' Jason inquired drily, nodding at the beach wrap, and Laura had to admit its folds were a little confining.

'I—I'll just put it over the back of the chair,' she murmured, slipping her arms out of the sleeves rather self-consciously. The simple one-piece maillot she was wearing was quite revealing, and she was still absurdly sensitive with him.

'So you decided to wear a bathing suit,' Jason remarked, pouring himself some orange juice, and she concentrated on the contents of her glass to evade his sardonic gaze.

'I could hardly come down without one,' she countered, when she had herself in control again, and he shrugged.

'Why not? That's one of the advantages about this place. It's completely private. Apart from Leah and the others, of course.'

'Apart from Leath and the others,' put in Laura quickly. 'We're not exactly on our own here, are we?'

His eyes lifted. 'Do you wish we were?'

'I didn't say that. I simply meant—I can hardly go around in the nude in the circumstances, can I?'

'Point taken.' Jason's smile was sardonic. 'I shall have to give them the day off.'

'Jason!' Laura breathed a little restrictedly, and struggling to remember exactly why she was there, she said, 'Can't we talk seriously? You've never told me what you said to Pamela before you brought her here.'

'You've never asked me.'

'I haven't had much chance.'

'I wouldn't say that.' Jason regarded her through his lashes. 'What do you want to know?'

Laura sighed. 'Did...did you tell her you knew Mike Kazantis?'

'I may have.'

'And did you tell her he was married?'

'Did you expect me to?'

Laura shook her head. 'I don't know. I don't know

how she's taking this…this change of scene. She seemed…contented enough last night.'

'And that bothered you?'

'No.' Laura spread her hands. 'I just want to know what will happen if Kazantis comes here.'

'He won't.'

'How can you be so sure?' Laura gazed at him. 'He is your sister's husband!'

'Irene knows how I feel about Kazantis,' responded Jason laconically.

'I don't.'

His eyebrows arched. 'Am I supposed to understand that?'

'You should.' Laura lifted one slim shoulder. 'How do you really feel about—about what's happened?'

'How do you think I feel?'

'Oh, stop talking in riddles!' Laura was unnerved. 'Do you believe Pamela?'

'The letters seem to prove it, don't they?'

Laura's eyes widened. 'She's shown you those?'

'Apparently.' He shrugged. 'I wasn't what she expected.'

'What do you mean?'

'Well…' Jason hesitated. 'She seemed to have gathered, from your conversation, that I was middle-aged and rather pedantic.' He made a careless gesture. 'Much like your employer in London, I guess.'

'Leave Pierce out of this.'

'Okay.' He studied her indignant face with gentle mockery. 'But, in spite of what was said on the yacht, you can't deny you hadn't elaborated on our relationship to her, had you? I think she had the impression I was doing this because your typing speeds were so good.'

Laura's lips parted. 'You didn't…you didn't…'

'...tell her what I really like about you?' inquired Jason lazily. 'That would have been indiscreet, wouldn't it she has no idea what a sexy...'

'Jason, please!' Laura interrupted him hotly, her cheeks burning, and his eyes dwelt with infuriating satisfaction on her agitated face. 'After—after what you said last night, you can hardly pretend your motives for bringing me here are in any way...emotional!'

'What did I say last night?'

'You know what you said.' She licked a drop of orange juice from her lip and faced him determinedly.

'That you were a hag?' he suggested softly, revealing he knew exactly what he had said, and Laura clenched her fists. 'I was angry. I say a lot of things when I'm angry. It doesn't follow that I mean them.'

Laura pressed her lips together. 'I think you did mean it.'

'You're determined to put words into my mouth. aren't you?' His eyes darkened. 'And you definitely don't look like a hag this morning. In fact, if I were a more fanciful man, I'd say you looked rather bewitching. You should wear your hair loose more often. I always preferred it that way.'

Laura looked down at her hands. 'If I'm going to spend any time out here, I may consider having it cut,' she said. 'It wasn't as long as this when...when I first came to the islands.'

'Don't!' Jason sobered, reaching towards her and winding a handful of its silken strands around his fingers. 'If you need to keep it in that braid for coolness, then okay. But don't cut it.'

It was a charged moment, and Laura felt the potent strength of his masculinity embracing her, surrounding her, *suffocating* her. Her breathing suspended, and she had to fight to hold on to her self-possession. The radiance of the morning, the pool and its colourful accoutrements; even the muted clamour of the ocean on the reef, all faded, replaced by the compelling brilliance of his eyes.

'I—that's my decision, Jason,' she got out finally, and the dark fringe of his lashes veiled his expression.

'Don't make me make it a condition, Laura,' he warned her roughly, tugging a little cruelly at her hair before releasing her, and she was still trying to control her agitation when she glimpsed a movement beyond the rigid contours of his face.

In the moment it took her to identify her sister's bikini-clad form, Jason sensed her sudden withdrawal. Glancing over his shoulder, he saw Pamela strolling in their direction, and his expression perceptibly hardened. 'Oh, beautiful,' he muttered, but it wasn't a compliment. More a bitter epithet that was accompanied by an even cruder expletive as he thrust back his chair and got to his feet.

'Oh…you're up, Laura.'

Pamela's response to her sister's presence was hardly flattering, but Laura was too relieved the other girl apparently hadn't overheard Jason's harsh profanity to feel indignant. Even so, it did occur to her that Pamela had spoken as if Laura's existence was not crucial to her being there, and it reminded Laura that, in spite of being sisters, it was some years since they had been really close. After all, Pamela had been only a teenager when she joined the staff of St Monica's as a probationary nurse. Now, almost twenty-five, she was very much a young woman, and Laura was being forced to regard her in quite a different light.

'Yes,' she answered now, still very much aware of

Jason's impatient stance beside her. 'I feel much better this morning. I'm sorry about last night. I must have seemed very rude.'

'Oh, forget it.' Pamela sank gracefully into the chair Jason had pulled out for her, smiling her thanks up at him. 'You really looked shattered. Thank goodness flying's never affected me in that way.'

'No...well...' Laura realised Jason was waiting for her response, and shifted a little uneasily. 'It was an extremely long journey.'

'Hmm.' Pamela shrugged. 'Not to worry. Jason and I had a cosy dinner together, didn't we?' This as Jason came round from behind her chair. 'I don't think he was too disappointed.'

Laura felt a twinge of something at this blatant attempt to exclude her, and she looked up at Jason sharply, wondering with a sudden hollowness, exactly what his feelings towards Pamela were. Was his resentment at Pamela's intervention what it seemed, or was he impatient with her for creating a situation he was not yet prepared to deal with? It was a development Laura had never anticipated—that Jason might be attracted to her sister—and she couldn't deny the fierce anger that gripped her at the thought.

'I guess we both made the best of it,' he responded now, meeting Laura's gaze without flinching. His smile was controlled. 'If you'll both excuse me, I have some telephone calls I want to make. Enjoy your breakfast. I'll see you later.'

Laura didn't know if it was her imagination, but the air seemed distinctly cooler after Jason had departed, and she was not entirely surprised when Pamela looked across at her with resentment marring her fair complexion.

'Why didn't you tell me?' she demanded, gazing at her sister with angry eyes. 'You must have known I would find out, sooner or later.'

'Tell you what?' inquired Laura, playing for time, and Pamela tapped her nails against the glass surface of the table in obvious frustration.

'Don't pretend you don't know what I mean!' she retorted. 'Although, if I hadn't heard it myself, I would never have believed it! You were Jason's mistress, weren't you? My God!' She shook her head. 'And I was afraid to tell you about Mike and me!'

Laura poured herself some coffee with more confidence than she had known she possessed. 'Is that an accusation?' she inquired, reaching for a *croissant*. 'I don't see that it affects you, one way or the other.'

'Don't you?' Pamela flung herself back in the chair, her jaw clenched sullenly. 'But that's why Jason agreed to have us here, isn't it? I just wonder how you forced him into this position. He must hate your guts!'

Laura continued to butter her croissant, even though her hands were shaking so much she could hardly hold the knife. It was hard to do anything in the face of such a scathing allegation, and for a few moments she was unable to speak at all. That her sister should believe *she* could force *Jason* to do anything? she thought, half hysterically. Obviously, Pamela had no idea of the character of the man they were dealing with.

'It's not your problem, Pam,' she managed to say at last choosing her words with care. 'You're here, aren't you? And on your own admission, you think this is a heavenly place. That's all that need concern you.'

'No, it's not.' Pamela regarded her sister without liking. 'I don't like the idea that—that I'm being *used* to get back at Jason for the way he treated you in the past!

I like him. I *really* like him. And I don't think it's fair
to expect him to support both of us!'

Laura was aghast. 'Pam…'

'I don't care what you say. I won't change my mind,'
retorted Pamela sulkily. 'If I'd known what was going
on before you left San Francisco, I'd have told you then.
As it is, I see no point in your staying on here until I
have the baby. It's not as if I need a chaperon, or anything. You can come and see the bungalow, if you like.
It's very self-contained. Once…once it's over, we can
talk again.'

Laura absorbed what the other girl was saying with a
feeling of disbelief. Was this really her younger sister
talking? Was this really the girl who, only two weeks
ago, was threatening to take her own life? What had
happened in the interim to change the situation so drastically? And what about the man who had fathered the
child she was carrying? Why had his name not even
been mentioned?

Jason!

Without needing to seek any further, Laura guessed
exactly why Pamela had lost all interest in Mike
Kazantis. Probably without even trying, Jason had driven
all thoughts of the other man out of her head, and
Laura's stomach contracted as her earlier fears were re-
kindled.

'Was—was it Jason who told you about—about our
relationship?' she ventured now, feeling her way, but
Pamela shook her head.

'Of course not,' she exclaimed scornfully. 'It's not
something he'd talk about, is it?' She shrugged. 'No. As
a matter of fact, it was Leah. I don't think she realised
I didn't already know about it.'

'Oh.' Laura breathed a little more easily.

Pamela went on, 'She asked if I'd ever visited the penthouse apartment in Honolulu, where you and he used to live?' Her lips twisted. 'Naturally, I said no. My God, it was all I could do not to ask her what the hell she was talking about! I'm glad I didn't. It was quite an education.'

Laura lifted one shoulder. 'I see.'

'Is that all you can say? *I see*?' Pamela stared at her angrily. 'Well? What are you going to do about it? Surely, you must see, you can't stay here now. It isn't fair on Jason, and it isn't fair on me.'

Laura moistened her lips. 'Why isn't it fair on you?'

'Well—well, because it isn't.'

'I gather you're not intending to leave, whatever happens,' Laura commented quietly, and Pamela had the grace to colour.

'I can't, can I?' she muttered reluctantly. 'I mean—it would be stupid!' She hesitated. 'Jason says that after I've had the baby, he might be able to find me a job here in Hawaii. It would be crazy to turn a chance like that down. Even you must see that.'

'And the baby?' Laura arched one brow. 'Have you decided what you're going to do about that?'

'Keep it, I suppose.' Pamela shrugged. 'There wouldn't be much point in my being here otherwise.'

'No.' Laura acknowledged this with some reluctance. But she couldn't help the unwilling suspicion that Pamela had weighed all the alternatives in the balance, and come up with the one that suited her best. And enabled her to stay here, on Jason's estate, added Laura silently.

'So...what are you going to do?'

Pamela had regained much of her self-confidence now, and she was evidently waiting for some reply. So

Laura gave her one. 'I suggest we leave the situation as it is for the time being,' she declared with determined brightness. Until she had spoken to Jason, she didn't want to get involved in any more argument. Ignoring Pamela's sulky features, she got up from her chair and sauntered with forced casualness to the edge of the patio. Shading her eyes for a moment, she looked at the ocean. 'I think I'll go for a swim. The water's deliciously cool at this time of day.' She glanced back at Pamela. 'You ought to try it.'

'If I want to swim, I'll swim in the pool,' retorted the other girl shortly. She paused. 'Do you intend to go on living in this house?'

Oh, really! Laura sighed. This was becoming ridiculous. 'What alternative do I have?' she demanded, in a driven tone, and Pamela rose to her feet.

'You could share the bungalow with me,' she replied at once. 'There are two bedrooms. You'd have plenty of room.'

'Then why don't you suggest that to Jason?' exclaimed Laura tersely, weary of trying to find excuses. 'I'm going down to the beach. You can tell Jason that, too, when you see him!'

CHAPTER NINE

LAURA WAS soaking in one of the twin tubs when a kind of sixth sense warned her she was no longer alone. Turning her head, she was hardly surprised to find Jason behind her, his shoulder propped indolently against the frame of the bathroom door. He was watching her, his eyes narrowed and intent, and her face suffused with colour at the arrogance of his appraisal.

'What do you want?' she asked, checking to make sure the water was lapping concealingly above her breasts, totally unaware that with her newly-washed hair wound into a careless knot on top of her head and her face flushed and defensive, she presented an infinitely provocative picture.

'What do you think I want?' inquired Jason, countering her question with one of his own. Then, less aggressively, he added: 'I came to find you. Pamela said you'd gone swimming, but evidently she was wrong.'

'I...did swim for a while,' said Laura quickly. 'But that was over an hour ago. And I wanted to rinse the salt off my skin.'

'Ah.' Jason nodded. 'Did you enjoy it?'

'Mmm.' Laura sighed reminiscently. 'It was beautiful!'

'Good.' He straightened away from the door and strolled across the marbled tiles with bare feet. 'So...are you ready to tell me what you've been telling your sister? She seems to think you've been blackmailing me.'

Laura bent her head, unknowingly exposing the sensitive curve of her nape, with its vulnerable curls of damp silk, to his gaze. 'Is that what she said?'

'As good as.' Jason squatted down beside her, his feet scarcely inches from the rim of the tub. 'Why didn't you tell her the truth?'

Laura lifted one slim shoulder, supremely conscious of his nearness. 'I don't think she'd have believed me,' she admitted honestly. She moistened her lips. 'You seem to have made another conquest!'

'Is that my fault, too?' Jason's arms were resting along his thighs, his knees wide apart, his whole attitude disturbingly sensual. And Laura was not unaware of it.

'I—perhaps not,' she murmured, flinching when he dipped one hand into the water and disturbed its protective surface.

'There's no ''perhaps'' about it,' retorted Jason, straightening abruptly. Wiping his damp fingers on the seat of his denim shorts, he regarded her broodingly. 'Your sister's being here suits *my* purpose: not hers.'

Laura drew a slightly unsteady breath. 'Did you tell her that?'

'I told her you would not be moving into the bungalow,' he responded grimly. 'If you want me to be more explicit, I can be. I just didn't know what crazy tale you'd been concocting for her benefit, and I didn't want to call you a liar!'

Laura swallowed. 'Am I supposed to thank you?'

'No!' Jason spoke aggressively. 'I guess she'll get the picture when I tell her I'm taking you with me to the mainland tomorrow.'

Laura's lips parted in consternation. 'Tomorrow!' she echoed aghast.

'Those calls I made,' Jason reminded her evenly.

'Loath as I am to uproot you again so soon, I do have to be in San Francisco tomorrow night.'

Laura's heart sank. The idea of more travelling, when she had hardly recovered from the journey from England was almost as daunting as what the trip would entail in other ways. Alone with Jason, she would have no chance to avoid him.

'Do...do I have to go?' she asked tentatively, glancing up into his hard handsome face. 'I mean—if it's a business trip...'

'I know exactly what you mean,' retorted Jason harshly. 'And yes, you *do* have to go. Now, I suggest you get out of that bath and come downstairs. Lunch will be ready soon, and Leah was asking after you. She was most concerned that you didn't eat dinner last night.'

Laura's lips pursed. 'Yes, *sir*,' she responded tautly, and Jason's jaw tightened as he met her resentful gaze.

'Do you want me, Laura?' he inquired with grim purpose, bending down to lift the burnished gold plug that released the water, and she watched with horrified eyes as the level in the bath began to fall.

'You—you have to be joking,' she exclaimed, presenting him with the downy curve of her back and rounded buttocks as she scrambled to reach a towel. 'Will you get out of here?' she added, grasping the fluffy apricot bathsheet and wrapping it closely about her. 'Am I to have no privacy, as well as no choice?'

'So long as you continue to antagonise me, why should I consider your feelings?' retorted Jason. Grasping one end of the towel, he dragged it savagely out of her grasp. 'You shouldn't arouse me if you're not prepared to take the consequences.'

'I didn't invite you to come in here,' Laura exclaimed,

as he stepped down into the rapidly draining tub and lifted her struggling body into his arms. 'Jason, don't do this!'

'Why not?' His eyes dwelt briefly on the parted curve of her mouth and against her will, she felt a tremor of emotion sweep through her. 'Why don't you yell for your sister?' he suggested thickly. 'Right now, I'd be happy to show her exactly what the situation is between us.'

'Let me go!' cried Laura in protest, but Jason wasn't listening to her. Almost without effort, he stepped out of the tub and carried her through to the bedroom, apparently uncaring of the fact that his feet were leaving damp patches on the carpet or that the loosened tendrils of Laura's hair were dripping wetly down his chest.

'Why do I always end up fighting you?' he demanded, dropping her down on to the bed, and Laura gazed up at him warily when he didn't immediately fling himself beside her. 'You know how I feel about you, and yet you persist in treating me like some kind of pervert! Does that give you some satisfaction? Do you like the idea of making me squirm?'

'I don't know what you—'

'Yes, you do,' he contradicted her harshly, sinking down on to the side of the bed. 'Last night you knew exactly what you were doing. It may please you to know I spent the hours you were sleeping catching up on the correspondence that had accumulated while I was away.'

Laura propped herself up on her elbows, more disturbed than she wanted to admit by his bitter confession. 'I...my hair's wet,' she murmured, not knowing how to answer him, and with a smothered oath, Jason bore her back against the jade satin.

'So what?' he muttered against her lips, the abrasive

hardness of his chest crushing her breasts. 'Your body's wet, too.' His hand slipped sensuously along her inner thigh. 'And God, Laura, don't stop me! Help me—'

His hand moved to the buttoned fastening of his shorts, and with the hungry possession of his mouth sending the blood flowing wildly through her veins, Laura sensed his impatience. No longer in control of her actions, her fingers moved intuitively to the recalcitrant button, loosening it swiftly and pressing down the zip, so that the tumescent strength of his manhood surged hotly into her hands.

'Oh, Jason,' she breathed, unable to deny her instinctive reactions to his powerful body, and with a groan, he thrust into her, filling her completely.

'God,' he said unsteadily, burying his face in the scented warmth of her neck. 'Don't tell me you don't want this, because I won't believe you!'

Laura couldn't answer him, and even had she been able to, she doubted she would have argued with him. As it was, the sensual probe of his tongue was like velvet in her mouth, and the mounting heat of his body was driving her almost to distraction.

With a moan of submission, she wound her arms around his neck. Then, surging towards him, she urged him on with little broken sounds of pleasure, until the sweating rhythm of their bodies reached the summit and beyond...

Jason was still sleeping when Laura went downstairs.

She had drowsed, too, but only for a few minutes, and when she eventually roused herself to an awareness of her surroundings, Jason was lying on his stomach beside her. One arm was resting across her breasts, his fingers coiled in the still-damp tangle of her hair, while his leg rested between hers, a possessive weight of bone and muscle.

Laura was curiously reluctant to move at all, despite the proof that once again he had demonstrated his authority over her. In other circumstances, she would have been quite content to remain where she was until the sexual languor left her. Jason was unknowingly vulnerable in his unconscious state, and the consuming passion of his lovemaking had made her relaxed and sleepy.

But the remembrance that Pamela was downstairs, no doubt drawing her own conclusions for their continued absence, drove Laura to an unwilling activity, and releasing herself carefully, she slid off the bed. Jason made some involuntary protest, but he didn't open his eyes, and she guessed his sleepless night was catching up on him. With a groan of exhaustion, he stretched more expansively on the mattress, and without stopping to consider her actions, Laura lifted the folds of the bedspread to cover his naked body. Even in sleep, he possessed a potent magnetism, and she had no wish for one of the young maids to come upon him in this state. She didn't examine her motives for feeling this way too closely however. If it was jealousy, she didn't want to know about it. All she did know was that Jason had been right earlier when he had said she wanted him. She wanted him still, if she was honest, she acknowledged, moistening her lips with a quivering tongue.

She dressed in a simple cotton vest and wrap-around skirt, both in the same shade of hot pink. She chose the vivid colour deliberately, in an effort to shake off the mood of desperation that had gripped her, ever since she had admitted to herself that her feelings for Jason were as ambiguous as ever. She didn't want to think about the implications of that admission, and she certainly didn't want to consider how Jason might react if he should discover her weakness. Somehow, she had to hold on to the reasons that had driven her away from Jason in the first place; not succumb to his practised charm that was as treacherous as it was hollow.

Laura found Pamela waiting for her in a sunlit room overlooking the terrace. Her sister had evidently been back to her bungalow to change her clothes, and now she was coolly elegant in a drop-waisted tunic made of blue and white striped linen. Looking at Pamela with objective eyes, Laura had to admit she was an attractive young woman. Tall, though perhaps not quite as tall as Laura, nevertheless she carried herself with confidence, her slim body showing no signs as yet of the reason she had appealed to her sister for help. Her hair, which had never aspired to the purity of Laura's, she had had tinted to an attractive tawny shade, and curling as it did about her ears, it softened the contours of her pointed features.

A table had been laid for lunch, and before Pamela could ask where Jason was, Leah appeared. 'So you decided to put in an appearance at last,' she remarked, with the familiarity of long service. 'Be thankful it's a cold meal. You have any idea how long it's been waiting?'

Laura felt her colour deepen, but she couldn't help it. 'I'm sorry, Leah,' she said, glancing awkwardly at her sister. 'And would you mind just serving two? Jason's asleep.'

'Is he?' Leah flicked a look from one to the other of them. 'Well, I do know he was up mighty early this morning.'

'That's right, he was.' Laura grasped the excuse with both hands. 'He—he's exhausted. I expect he'll get something later, when he wakes up.'

'Good enough.'

Leah seemed satisfied with this explanation, but after the two girls were seated at the table, Pamela regarded her sister with less conviction. 'Jason told me you wouldn't be moving into the bungalow,' she remarked tersely. 'Do you mind telling me why? Just so I don't make any more gaffes where you're concerned.'

Laura sighed. 'It's a long story, Pam. I'd rather not go into it right now.'

'Why not?'

'Well, is it important?'

'It is to me.' Pamela forked a slice of marinated cucumber into her mouth. 'If you and Jason still have a thing for one another, I'd like to know why you haven't seen one another for the past three years.'

'We don't still have "a thing" for one another,' retorted Laura swiftly, eager to stifle the thought before it could take root. After the anxiety of her own thoughts upstairs, she had no wish for Pamela to put into words something she could not—and would not—acknowledge. 'I can't explain. Just take my word that Jason is only helping us because it suits him to do so.'

Pamela looked thoughtful. 'I see.' She paused. 'But your being here is part of the deal.'

'Yes.' Laura expelled her breath with relief. She had not expected it to be so easy. Pouring herself a glass of orange juice, she raised it to her lips and thirstily drained it. 'I'm glad you understand.'

Pamela frowned. 'Just one thing.'

'Yes?' Laura was wary.

'When you and Jason split up—whose fault was that?'

Laura inwardly groaned. Obviously her relief had been premature. 'Does it matter?' she asked, refilling her glass. 'We had a—a difference of opinion. These things happen. It was no one's—fault.'

'It must have been some difference of opinion for you to give up your life out here,' remarked Pamela impatiently. She hesitated. 'Was someone else involved?'

'I'd really rather not talk about it, Pam.'

'But you must admit it's an odd situation,' exclaimed her sister frustratedly. 'I mean—if it was Jason who was playing around, why should he be willing to help us now? And why should you even think he might? You did approach him, didn't you? It wasn't the other way about.'

'Jason has his own reasons for doing things,' replied Laura wearily. 'He likes—manipulating people. I don't know why I thought he might be willing to help us. I suppose because he was the only person I could think of who could.'

Pamela absorbed this, and then she said shrewdly: 'Why don't you admit it, Laura. You walked out on Jason. I guess you found him with some other woman, or something equally as petty. My God! Imagine giving all this up! You must have been crazy!'

Laura wondered anew at her ignorance of her sister's character. When had the confiding teenager she remembered turned into this cynical adult? 'The reasons I left Jason were not petty!' she retorted, stung into retaliation. 'The advantages of wealth are not a precept for happiness!'

Pamela grimaced. 'Don't be pompous, Laura. We're not all as sanctimonious as you are. However, you have reassured me. I don't like stepping on anyone's toes, and as you don't want Jason, you can't blame me if I don't share your views. It seems to me, you've had it your own way far too long, and if it's happened before, it can happen again. I'm quite prepared to settle for a man, not a saint.'

*   *   *

Laura spent the afternoon with Leah, trying unsuccessfully to escape from the memory of that distasteful scene with her sister. To her relief, Pamela had returned to her own bungalow after lunch, and Laura sought Leah's company in an effort to restore her sense of balance.

To begin with, her conversation with Jason's housekeeper bore the strains of her own tortured nerves, and she would not have blamed Leah if she had made the wrong connection. After all, she was fiercely protective of Jason's interests, and she had every reason to distrust the English girl after what had happened. But if the Polynesian woman felt any resentment, she did not openly display it, and inevitably Laura's agitation eased in Leah's undemanding presence.

After taking the girl on a conducted tour of the ground floor of the house, Leah invited her into the kitchen. Like the other rooms, this too was light and airy, and after seating her guest on a padded bamboo stool, the housekeeper produced a jug of strawberry daiquiris from the refrigerator.

'Oh, I don't know,' murmured Laura doubtfully, when Leah set a tall glass overflowing with slices of fruit and topped with a pale pink blossom in front of her. 'I don't usually drink in the afternoons. As a matter of fact, I don't usually drink much at all.'

'Lighten up,' advised Leah drily, pouring herself a glass of the same. 'You look as if you need it. Why do I get the feeling that it's you, and not your sister, who needs Jason's help?'

Laura sighed. 'I'm all right.'

'Are you?' Leah regarded her doubtfully. 'You know, when Jason said he was bringing you here, I thought he was a fool! And I said so. When you walked out on him, I thought if I ever saw you again I'd want to black your eye. But, Jason made me promise not to upset you, and when I saw you yesterday afternoon, I knew why he said it.'

'Oh, Leah!'

'I know, I know. You don't want to talk about it. And I'm not going to go back on my word. But, if you've got any sense, you'll hang in there this time. Whatever his faults, and I'm not saying he's without any, Jason's a good man. He wouldn't hurt you like you hurt him.'

'Want to bet?' Laura moved half a strawberry aside and took a sip of the cocktail. 'Mmm, this is delicious!' she murmured obliquely. 'Why do your daiquiris always taste so much better than anyone else's?'

'I guess it's a natural talent,' responded Leah wryly, noticing the change of topic. 'I tell you what, hon—next time I make some, you can watch me.' She paused. 'I know exactly how Jason likes them.'

Laura sighed. 'You've been with him a lot of years, haven't you, Leah? I don't suppose anyone knows him better than you do.'

'I wouldn't say that.' Leah looked at the younger woman out of the corners of her eyes. 'I thought you knew him pretty well, Laura. At least better than any of the other girls he's known.'

'And he's known a lot,' put in Laura bitterly. 'You can't deny that.'

Leah shrugged. 'Some,' she conceded carelessly. 'They didn't mean anything.'

'Oh, come on.' The alcohol in the daiquiri was giving Laura more confidence. 'What about Regina? He married her!'

'Regina!' The way the housekeeper said the other woman's name was scathing. 'You want to know about

Regina? Girl, you know he never cared about that Italian bitch!'

Laura licked her lips. 'You don't really know that, Leah. I know you've said it before, but really you're only guessing.'

'Who? Me?' Leah was indignant. 'Jason married Regina to please his family. Believe it! I wouldn't lie to you.'

Laura shook her head. Once, perhaps, she had believed her, but not now. Once, she had had aspirations in that direction herself, and she had believed anyone who told her Jason's reputation was not what it appeared. It had seemed quite reasonable to put his single venture into matrimony down to a family commitment, and even the fact that Regina had divorced him had not really been a cause for concern. Now, however, she had her own painful experiences to guide her, and Leah's well-rehearsed reassurance had little power to convince.

'Leah, Jason wouldn't marry anyone just to please his family,' she declared now, wondering why the juicy piece of fruit from her glass suddenly tasted so sour. 'He's not that kind of man. You know it, and I know it. So, let's stop pretending, shall we?'

Leah regarded the girl with some uncertainty, and then she said heavily: 'You didn't use to be so bitter, girl. What have you been doing since you made off back to England?'

Laura shrugged. 'This and that. I'm a secretary now, to a famous thriller writer. It's very interesting work. It's quite different from anything else I've ever done.'

Leah frowned. 'This writer—he's a man?'

'Pierce Carver, yes.'

'Are you involved with him?'

'Leah!'

The housekeeper grimaced. 'I'm just trying to find out why you've gotten so hard, Laura,' she declared flatly. 'For someone who walked out on Jason, you're pretty sore towards him, aren't you?'

Laura sighed. 'Leah, I'd really rather not talk about that.'

'I know, I know.' Leah sniffed. 'You just want to go on, believing the worst of him!'

Laura bent her head. 'You could be right.'

'Well, it isn't fair.'

'Fair?' Laura's head jerked up. 'Leah, what are you trying to say? When was Jason ever fair—with anyone? Including Regina.'

Leah hesitated. 'What if I was to tell you the real reason Jason married Regina? The reason why he and his Daddy don't see one another any more?'

Laura gasped. 'Leah, you're priceless…'

'No, I mean it.' Leah looked unusually sombre. 'I was told never to talk about it, but…'

'Leah, stop it!' Laura's patience was stretched. 'Look, I understand your loyalty towards him, and I know he would never do anything to hurt you, but isn't this carrying things a little too far? I mean, when it comes to inventing stories…'

'It's no invention.' Leah was indignant. 'Jason's father wasn't always as successful as he is now. There was a time when he'd have done anything to make a dollar— including marrying his own son to the daughter of one of his most powerful enemies!'

'Oh, really?' Laura was openly incredulous. 'I understood Regina was a model.'

'So she was.' Leah considered her words before continuing: 'But she was also Paulo Enrico's daughter.'

Laura gazed impatiently at her. 'Are you really telling me that Regina's family are as wealthy as the Montefiores?'

'They get along.'

'Do they?'

'Listen…' Leah glanced about her apprehensively, as if suspecting someone might be eavesdropping on their conversation, and then added huskily, 'Marco—that's Jason's father…'

'I know.'

'…he had gotten involved in some deal that didn't work out. He was in hock—*debt*—to the tune of some ten million dollars. Not a lot by today's standards, maybe, but sufficient to put his company in danger of collapse. He needed the money. Enrico provided it.'

'Just like that.' Laura was sardonic.

'There were conditions.'

Laura grimaced. 'Jason's marriage to Regina?' She shook her head. 'If the two men were enemies, as you say, why should this man, Enrico, want Jason to marry his daughter?'

'I don't guess he did.' Leah sniffed. 'But Regina wanted Jason. And she got him.'

'How sweet!' Laura didn't believe a word of it. 'And that's why Jason doesn't speak to his father.'

'That's part of it.'

Laura finished her drink and set the glass down again rather heavily. 'So tell me, if Regina's family are so wealthy, why is she constantly coming to Jason for money?'

'If you think that's why she comes to Jason, you're a fool,' retorted Leah shortly. 'And the rest of the story isn't so pretty. But forget it! I've said too much as it is.'

'Oh, you have.' Laura slipped off the stool to face her. 'Leah, I know you mean well, and I do appreciate your—your confidence. But Jason has his own rules. And—and so do I.'

Laura had tea on the patio alone, and then went for a walk along the beach. It was so peaceful there, with only the surf and the wind soughing through the palms to keep her company. She didn't want to go back to the suite while Jason was sleeping, but when she eventually returned to the house, she found him lounging on the low wall that circled the terrace, evidently waiting for her. He was dressed now, in close fitting cream cotton pants and a knitted cashmere sweater, and Laura couldn't help the sharp contraction of her stomach at his unconscious sexuality.

He got to his feet at her approach, and stepped aside when she made to go up to the terrace. But, before she could avoid a confrontation, his fingers closed about her forearm. 'I wanted to tell you,' he said. 'Before your sister gets here, and before we get bogged down in the kind of small talk women seem to think is so important. I've changed my mind about tomorrow.'

For a moment, Laura's mind went blank. After the conversation she had had with Leah, her head had been filled with other things, and she could only stare at him. 'Tomorrow?'

'Our proposed trip to San Francisco,' said Jason flatly. 'Remember?'

Laura stiffened. 'It's not something I'd forget,' she lied. 'What is there to say?'

Jason released her arm and pushed his hands into the waistband of his pants. 'I've decided not to take you with me,' he declared without emotion. His eyes probed hers. 'Much as I shall miss the stimulation of your company, the violent nature of our—relationship, shall we say—could prove something of a distraction. And it is a business trip, after all.'

Laura couldn't speak. It should have been what she wanted; it should have been a source of some relief that she was not to be expected to play a role that was abhorrent to her. But it wasn't. What she truly felt was a sense of bereavement, and when she did find words to answer him, they mirrored her pained frustration.

'So who is going with you?' she inquired tightly. 'Or is that a leading question? Why don't you take Pamela? I believe she wouldn't object.'

Jason stared at her with cold assessing eyes. 'I believe you could be right,' he responded harshly. 'Though why it should give you so much pleasure to say so, I can't imagine. However, loath as I am to refute that damning opinion you have of me, I am going without female companionship!'

Laura quivered. 'You surprise me.'

'Yes.' Jason's jaw clenched. 'I surprise myself sometimes. Not least, when I continue to want you, even when I know you really hate my guts!'

CHAPTER TEN

LAURA DID NOT speak to Jason again before he left. Contrary to her expectation, he made no attempt to invade her rooms after she had retired for the night, and she learned the next morning that the plane she had heard taking off soon after midnight, had in fact had Jason as its passenger. He had apparently decided to take advantage of an overnight flight, and she assumed his early departure would precipitate his eventual homecoming.

In the days that followed whenever she heard the sound of an aircraft overhead, she expected it to be Jason. But the days stretched into a week, and then into two, and still he did not return. If Leah had heard from him, she did not say, and Laura was too proud to ask the housekeeper for information. Instead, she endeavoured to create a pattern for her days, and did her best to maintain a relationship with her sister, although that wasn't always easy.

For her part, Pamela seemed to have adapted very well to her new surroundings. Lazing in the sun; splashing about in the pool; occasionally joining Laura on one of her frequent walking expeditions—she seemed happiest doing nothing at all, and Laura found it simpler to avoid talking about the future. Now and then, Jason's name would be mentioned, usually by Pamela and usually concerning his prolonged absence. But generally their conversations encompassed impersonal things, and Laura suspected Pamela was as unwilling as herself to discuss Jason's possible intentions.

Even so, as each succeeding day went by, Laura found her own emotions less easy to control. In spite of assuring herself that she was glad of his absence, it simply wasn't possible to sustain that belief after she got to bed at night; and sleeping in his house, and his rooms, and his *bed*, made a difficult situation unbearable. Wherever she looked, she was reminded of him; his shaving equipment was in one of the glass cabinets in the bathroom; his hair brushes resided on a tray in the dressing room; his clothes hung in the closet opposite hers. Even the fragrant aroma of the sheets reminded her of him, and more than one night she had awakened to find herself clutching his pillow to her chest. The fact that the pillow, too, had been damp with tears was another cause for self-condemnation.

In consequence when, fifteen days after his departure, the Learjet flew in low over the island, she could hardly wait for one of the servants to go the airport to meet him. Had it not been for Pamela's curious eyes upon her, Laura knew she would have offered to go and meet Jason herself, but instead she was forced to wait, tense and nervous, until the familiar sound of the automobile was heard from the front of the house. She didn't know what she was going to say to him; she didn't even know how she would react when she saw him; she only knew she had missed him more than she would have thought possible, and her blood raced hotly at the realisation that the aching need she had hardly suppressed was soon to be assuaged.

It was late afternoon when Laura heard the sound she had been waiting for, and abandoning any attempt at hiding her relief, she got hurriedly to her feet. Because Pamela was with her, she had not had an opportunity to change her clothes, but the loose-fitting sleeveless smock, worn over baggy Bermudas, was not unattractive. Although the two shades of rose-pink did not exactly match, they blended well together, and accentuated the pale tan that covered her bare arms and legs. Her hair was in its usual thick braid, but she could loosen that later. When she and Jason were alone, she thought unsteadily, as she walked along the terrace and turned the corner of the house.

The cream convertible was where she expected it to be, but as she started eagerly towards it, her steps faltered. It was not Jason who was getting out of the passenger seat, and she fell back into the shadows as a young woman wearing tightly-fitting white jeans and a black blouson appeared. Her hair was dark and curly, and its expertly-cut style framed her narrow face with provocative tendrils, She was quite tall, and slim, and from the familiar way she was speaking to Jonah, it was not her first visit to the island. Who was she? Laura wondered faintly, a hollow emptiness replacing her earlier anticipation. Another of Jason's women, come to view the opposition? Or the reason for his prolonged absence—his next move in his plans to humiliate her?

'Who is she?'

Unaware, Pamela had followed her, and now Laura had to steel her features before turning to face her sister. 'How should I know?' she responded tensely, eager now to get out of sight. 'Why don't you ask her?'

'*Laura!*'

Their brief exchange had apparently attracted the girl's attention, and Laura knew a hopeless sense of frustration as the newcomer turned from directing Jonah's efforts with her luggage to come towards them. Just for that moment, the fact that the girl knew her name hardly registered. All Laura could think of was that once again she had been a fool—that Jason cared no more for her now than he had ever done.

'Laura!' the girl said again, less confidently now, and although there was still at least fifty feet between them, suddenly Laura knew who it was.

'Lucy?' she ventured disbelievingly, and then more strongly, 'Lucy, is it really you?' She shook her head. 'Dear God! I wouldn't have recognised you!'

Ignoring Pamela's terse: 'Who is Lucy?' Laura abandoned her reserve and rushed down the steps to meet Jason's daughter halfway. 'Oh, Lucy!' she exclaimed, feeling the girl's arms close around her and the dampness of uncontrollable tears on her own cheeks. 'I'm sorry. I thought you were someone else!'

'Who?' demanded Lucy at last, pulling back to look at the girl she had come to regard with affection. Before Laura walked out on her father, they had become the best of friends, but like the other people who knew him, Jason's daughter was now looking at her with some suspicion. 'Who were you expecting?'

'Oh—no one—I mean—well, Jason, I suppose,' murmured Laura unhappily. Then, surveying the young woman facing her with some amazement, she added, 'When did you grow up?'

'You have been gone three years, Laura,' Lucy pointed out drily. 'I'm nearly eighteen. Not a child any more.'

'I can see that.' Laura held her at arm's length and smiled. 'You're quite—beautiful! I'm sure your father would agree.'

'Do you think so?' Lucy's instinctive plea for reassurance was very childlike suddenly, but then her dark eyes narrowed. 'Oh—was that what you thought? That I was one of Daddy's girlfriends? Yes. Yes, I can see that you did. Shame on you, Laura. He's really not like that. I thought you knew.'

Laura's hands dropped. 'Oh…I…don't be silly, Lucy. Why should it matter to me if your father brings a woman here? Didn't he tell you? I'm only here because of my sister. Where is he, by the way? Did you leave him at the airport?'

'Daddy?' Lucy shook her head. 'He's not here.'

'He's not!' Laura managed to control the incipient catch in her voice. 'Wh…where is he?'

'In Honolulu, I think,' replied Lucy carelessly. He told me to tell you his business is taking longer than he thought.' She looked beyond Laura and frowned. 'Is that your sister—over there?'

'Oh yes.' Laura gathered herself with an effort, and turned. 'Come and meet her.' She moistened her lips. 'Pam—this is Jason's daughter, Lucia. Lucy—this is Pam.'

'Jason's daughter?' Pamela gazed at the girl disbelievingly. 'I didn't even know he was married!'

'He's not.' Lucy answered her. 'He and my mother were divorced almost fifteen years ago. But—Laura and I are old friends.'

'Really?' Pamela arched her dark brows. 'How nice.'

'Yes, isn't it?' Despite her youth, Lucy had already sensed the other girl's hostility. Tucking her arm through Laura's, she led her up the steps. 'Come and talk to me while I change. I can't wait to get into my bikini.'

While Lucy spoke with the maid over where she wanted her suitcases unpacking, Laura leaned on the balcony rail, trying to come to terms with the fact that Jason would not be returning in the foreseeable future. Was that why he had sent his daughter here? she wondered. So that Lucy could keep an eye on her? However uncharitable this notion might be, she could not dismiss it, and she turned to look down at the patio, biting her lips in raw frustration.

Pamela had returned to her seat by the pool, she noticed, her sister's slim form visible beyond the sheltering canopy of a striped umbrella. Obviously she was not going to allow Lucy's arrival to upset her, and Laura half envied Pamela's ability to think only of herself.

'She's not at all like you, is she?' remarked Lucy, in her ear, and Laura turned to find the younger girl had shed her jeans and blouson and was standing unashamedly in only a lace-trimmed pair of panties. 'Is she really in love with Uncle Mike? She doesn't look very heart-broken to me.'

Laura walked back into the bedroom, as much to prevent Pamela from overhearing their conversation as a need to remind Lucy that she might be observed by one of the servants. 'Your father told you about that, hmm?' she murmured, taking hold of one of the carved posts that were set at each of the four corners of the bed.

'No. It was Nonna, actually.' Lucy slipped the narrow bra of a white bikini over her small breasts. Then her fingers moved to the buttoned fastening of her panties. 'She asked me if I had seen you since you came back. She wanted to know what my father plans to do.'

'I see.' Laura's palms felt moist against the polished wood. 'And what else did your grandmother say? Does she intend to tell Irene when she gets back from Italy?'

Lucy stepped into white bikini pants. 'Since when did Aunt Irene go to Italy?' she asked, surveying her reflection in a long antique mirror. 'She's at home right now. Daddy had dinner with her the other evening.'

'He did?' Laura looked blank. 'But I thought...'

Lucy frowned. 'Did Daddy tell you Aunt Irene was in Italy?'

Laura bent her head. 'I thought he did.'

'Oh, well—' Lucy shrugged. 'It's no big deal, is it? I guess he forgot—or was mistaken, or something.'

'Yes.' Laura appeared to accept the girl's explanation but inside she was a mass of conflicting thoughts and emotions. Why would Jason lie about a thing like that? Unless…unless, he had intended to prevent her from contacting Mike Kazantis. Would he go so far to protect his sister? She thought he would.

'Anyway, Nonna was surprised when Daddy told her you were back.' Lucy grimaced. 'I was, too, but probably not for the same reasons.'

'What do you mean?' Laura was intrigued in spite of herself.

'Oh…' Lucy shrugged, and turned away from her reflection without conceit. 'I always knew Daddy wanted you back. Heavens,' she grimaced, 'you couldn't live with him after you went away!'

Laura bent her head. 'I think you're exaggerating.'

'No, I'm not.' Lucy was indignant. 'You knew how he felt about you. I almost hated you for what you did to him!'

Laura drew an uneven breath. 'You don't understand…'

'No, I don't.' Lucy squared her shoulders. 'Like I said, I was pretty mad when you walked out on him.' She shrugged. 'But then—I figured, it must be something pretty important for you to fade out of that kind of a relationship. I mean—I thought you were crazy about him, I really did. But when you left…' She shook her head. 'I never expected you'd come back.'

'Nor did I,' said Laura painfully, wishing she had

never started this. 'So…what was so different about you and your grandmother?'

'Nonna didn't know the way it was.'

Laura's brows drew together. 'The way it was?'

'Yes. Sure.' Lucy lifted her shoulders defensively. 'She…well, she thought my father made the break. She didn't discuss it with him. She never would. And I…well, I guess I let her go on thinking it.'

'Ah!' Laura nodded. 'That's why she was so surprised.'

'Yes.' Lucy inclined her head. 'I'm sorry.'

'Don't be.' Laura was quick to reassure her. 'It's not important.' She hesitated. 'But you didn't tell me what your grandmother said. Does—Aunt Irene know about… about what happened?'

'You mean you and Daddy?'

'No. I mean your Uncle Mike and Pamela,' responded Laura patiently. 'Did your father discuss it with her?'

'Oh, I don't know.' Lucy looked confused. 'Uncle Mike is always in trouble of some kind or another. He and Aunt Irene don't live together any more. They separated six months ago.'

'*Separated*!'

'They're still married, of course. But that's more because of the children than anything else. They live with Aunt Irene. Did you ever meet my cousins?'

Laura blinked. 'I…I may have done…'

'There are four of them, you know. Dino and Tina—they're the twins—they're sixteen. And Marco; he's twelve; and the youngest Sophia, she's seven.'

Laura shook her head. 'And your father knew this?'

'What?'

'That Mike Kazantis and his sister were separated.'

'I guess.' Lucy pulled a face. 'It's not a secret.'

'No.' Laura managed to put on a brave face. 'I've obviously misunderstood.'

'Hmm.' Lucy was unaware of the bombshell she had dropped. She turned back to her reflection. 'Do you think I look all right? You don't think this suit is just a bit— well, out-of-date?'

'Out of date?' echoed Laura blankly. 'I—not to me, Lucy. Could you wear anything less?'

Lucy giggled. 'You wouldn't believe it!' Then, she sobered again. 'Say—are you all right, Laura? I mean— you look kind of…stunned. What did I say?'

'Nothing. Nothing at all.' Laura managed to convince the girl that she was mistaken. 'So, when is your father coming back? Or is that a closely-guarded secret, too?'

'Too?' Lucy picked up on the word, but then she shrugged. 'I'm not sure. In a few days, I guess. Why don't you ring him? I can give you the number of his suite at the Ilikai.'

Laura was tempted. Her sense of frustration at the realisation that Jason had been lying to her all along was such that she longed to confront him with his duplicity. But the telephone was such an unsatisfactory way to conduct any kind of argument, and she wanted to see his face when she told him she knew what he had done.

'It's all right, Lucy,' she responded now, realising she could not involve Jason's daughter in this affair. 'I can wait. Now, why don't we go down and have some tea? Or perhaps you would prefer something cooler?'

In the days that followed, Laura became the unwilling recipient of many more confidences. Lucy seemed to think that Laura's return was permanent, and Laura could hardly disillusion her without involving herself in explanations she had no wish to share. In consequence,

Lucy began to treat her like a member of the family, and Laura was forced to listen, particularly when the girl spoke of her mother.

'She got married again, you know,' she remarked a couple of mornings later, as they sunbathed on the beach. It was early, too early for Pamela to join them, even had she wanted to, and Laura had noticed that Lucy seemed to enjoy these times best. 'My stepfather's an oil man; Ellis Hammond, have you heard of him? No? Well, you've probably heard of his company: Hamco.'

Laura frowned. 'When did she get married?'

'About two years ago.' Lucy grimaced. 'I guess, when she finally accepted that Daddy wasn't about to renew her contract.'

Laura stared at her. 'What do you mean?'

'Oh, you know!' Lucy sighed. 'She's been angling for him to remarry her for years. Surely you knew that.'

Laura wondered exactly how much she had known of the man she had lived with for more than two years. She shook her head. 'I didn't think of it.' She hesitated, and then added reluctantly: 'After all, your mother did divorce your father, didn't she? Not the other way around.'

'Oh, that!' Lucy was scathing. 'That was just so there was no hassle over my custody. Daddy could have divorced my mother half a dozen times over. It wasn't exactly a love-match—on his side, at least.'

Laura expelled her breath carefully. 'You're very cynical.'

'Wouldn't you be? For years my mother used me to get back at Daddy. If it hadn't been for you and Nonna, I'd have thought all wives acted that way.'

'Oh, Lucy…'

'No, it's true.' Lucy ran restless fingers through her

damp curls. 'I used to dread going to the office. I used to dread being unloaded like a sack of potatoes.'

'Oh, Lucy, your father always cared about you, you know that.'

'Well, yes. I guess he did. But until you went to live at the apartment, I never felt at home there.'

Laura bent her head. 'Thank you.'

'I mean it. Those other women…' She flushed as she realised what she had said; but Laura urged her to go on: 'Well—there were other women—but they meant nothing to him. They were just—there. You were different.'

'Was I?' Laura's tone was ironic, and Lucy frowned.

'You know you were,' she exclaimed fiercely. 'You're here, aren't you?'

Laura shrugged. 'For the present.'

'What do you mean?'

Lucy looked anxious, and Laura found herself reassuring her. 'Who knows?' she said, making light of her words. 'Who can foretell the future?'

Lucy still looked doubtful. 'You know—Daddy never talks about why you and he split up.' She paused, and then added softly: 'Why did you?'

'It's a long story.' Laura had suspected this was coming and now she reached purposefully for her towel. 'I'll tell you some day.'

'Why not now?'

'Because, like I said, it's a long story.'

'We've got time.'

'Oh, Lucy…'

'I know it had something to do with the Ridgeways, didn't it?' Lucy burst out, before the other girl could get to her feet, and Laura gazed at her, dry-mouthed.

'You know?'

'My mother told me,' admitted Lucy unhappily. Then, realising she had to say more, she went on: 'It was something to do with Ellen Ridgeway, wasn't it? Mom said that Daddy threw you over for her, but I didn't believe it!'

Laura's shoulders sagged. 'What else did your mother tell you?' she demanded heavily.

'Not much.' Lucy coloured. 'Was that it? Was that why you walked out? Because you thought Daddy was having an affair?'

Laura expelled her breath wearily. 'I suppose that sounds pretty stupid to you, hmm?' she inquired flatly.

'Stupid?' Lucy looked troubled.

'Yes.' Laura shrugged. 'You said yourself your father always had women around.'

'Not when he was with you?' exclaimed Lucy defensively. 'I told you...'

'But your mother seems to have thought he was involved with Ellen Ridgeway, doesn't she?'

'She would.' Lucy was impatient. 'Did she tell you that? Was that why you left?'

Laura shook her head. 'I wouldn't have believed anything your mother told me.' She grimaced. 'Perhaps I was wrong.'

'No, you weren't wrong.' Lucy was fierce in her father's defence. 'And if he was involved with Ellen Ridgeway, why didn't he go on seeing her, after you went back to England?'

'How do you know he didn't?'

Lucy gasped. 'Because I do. I was with him for most of that year. There were no other women.'

Laura plucked at the hem of the towel pressed against her chest. 'I imagine even your father has some sense of decency,' she declared tensely. 'I'd really rather not talk about it.'

'But you have to talk about it,' protested Lucy. 'If Daddy knew how you felt, he would want you to.'

'Would he?' Laura doubted it. Her feelings concerning Ellen and Jeff Ridgeway had never concerned him. 'Well—shall we go back? It's almost time for breakfast, and I'm ready for some coffee.'

Lucy followed her example and got to her feet, but her expression was still anxious. 'You won't…you won't tell Daddy I've said anything, will you?' she ventured awkwardly. 'He…he wouldn't like to think that Mom had—had discussed it with me.'

'Don't worry,' said Laura gently. 'It's unlikely to come up. So far as the Ridgeway deal is concerned, it's a closed book.'

Lucy had not said how long she planned to stay, and Laura did not like to ask her, in case the girl thought she wanted her to leave. In fact, Laura was glad of her company to ease the situation between herself and Pamela, which had not improved in the weeks since Jason had gone away. Laura sometimes wondered if her sister thought of Mike Kazantis at all, as she lay sunning herself beside Jason's pool. She had evidently resigned herself to his disappearance, but had she forgotten it was his child she carried?

Lucy, she knew, regarded the other girl with some resentment, but she knew better than to anger her father by getting involved. Nevertheless, she found it hard to understand why Laura hadn't just told Pamela who Mike Kazantis was.

'I mean,' she said one afternoon, as they drove into the village so that she could post a letter to her mother, 'it's not as if it's your fault that Uncle Mike is married to Daddy's sister. And as you did come to Daddy for help...'

Laura sighed. 'Pamela was...unstable at that time, Lucy,' she said unwillingly. 'Didn't your grandmother tell you that?'

'About her OD-ing?' Lucy grimaced. 'Oh, yes, she told me. But she doesn't really seem the type, does she?'

Laura shrugged. 'She was desperate. We all do things when we're desperate that aren't exactly typical.'

'Like you walking out on Daddy, hmm?' suggested Lucy slyly, as Laura parked the car in front of the little post office. 'I'm so glad you came back. I can forgive Pamela for almost anything for bringing that about.'

CHAPTER ELEVEN

LAURA ROLLED OVER in the bed and stretched tiredly. It was morning at last, she saw, grateful for the sun's rays slatting through the blind. She was not sleeping at all well, and the evening before she had swallowed several large daiquiris to ensure herself of a good night. But she had not had a good night. She had been hot and restless, and there had been times when she had imagined she was not alone in the big bed. She had felt the warmth of someone's body close to hers, and once she could have sworn warm lips had caressed the corner of her mouth. But she knew she had only been fantasizing, and her cheeks were still smudged with the tears she had shed in that unconscious state. It was frightening to realise how, even in her sleep, thoughts of Jason dominated her. Particularly, after what he had done—not just now, but three years ago...

She had not been lying when she told Lucy she had not believed anything her mother had said. Regina had always been jealous of her. She had known that. Although she had not really understood why until Lucy explained about her parents' divorce. Nevertheless, what she had not said was that Regina's malicious gossip had confirmed something Laura already knew to be true, and it was partly because of Regina's influence that she had run away from the situation.

But, Ellen Ridgeway had not lied to her. With her husband's body lying dead in his coffin, she had been too distraught to think of prevarication. Her white face, her tears; the haunting fear of guilt in her eyes, had all told their own story, and nothing could alter the fact that Jeff Ridgeway had killed himself because of his wife's involvement with Jason Montefiore. He had been a successful businessman, with companies not just here, in the islands but on the mainland, too. He had had no other reason to take his life, except that his wife was more than thirty years his junior and had evidently been cheating on him with a younger man.

All the pieces had fit. During that last month, Jason had paid unusually frequent visits to the mainland, leaving Laura alone in the apartment, even though she had been willing to go with him.

'It's business,' he had said. 'You'd be bored.' And Laura had believed him, because to her knowledge he had never lied to her before.

Even now, she could still remember the shock she had had when she had discovered Jason was not in San Francisco at all, but right there, in Honolulu. It was quite by chance she had seen him and Ellen Ridgeway together. She seldom left the apartment for meals, when she was on her own, but one fateful afternoon she had been invited, by one of the girls she used to work with at the agency, to a wedding shower they were giving for a girl who was leaving. It was to be held in the Colony Room of one of the larger Waikiki hotels, and when Laura walked into the discreetly-lit restaurant, the first person she saw was Jason, seated intimately in a booth with Ellen Ridgeway.

She shivered, remembering the chilling feeling of enlightenment that had swept over her at that moment. It was so unexpected; yet so predictable; and she had turned and walked out of the hotel again, without even hearing the puzzled reaction of her friends. She should have known it would happen sooner or later, she had told herself, as she walked blindly down the marble steps and out of the foyer. The miracle was it had taken so long. Jason's women seldom lasted longer than a couple of months, whereas she had lived with him for almost two years.

Jason had caught up with her in Kalakaua Avenue. She didn't know what excuse he had offered Ellen Ridgeway, and she didn't care, but the anger in his dark face prevented her from saying what she felt. 'It's not what you think,' he had declared roughly. 'I can't explain right now but you've got to trust me!'

And she had, even then, albeit with some misgivings. She had been so much in love with him, she would have believed anything at that moment, anything that would restore the relationship she had thought they shared. Even when, two days later, Jeff Ridgeway had leapt from the twenty-first floor of his hotel complex, she had sought for reasons that did not implicate Jason, striving desperately not to believe what was staring her in the face.

She didn't know why she had attended the funeral. Jason had not asked her to go. On the contrary, since Jeff Ridgeway's suicide, he had been curiously remote, and Laura had had no chance to question him, even had she felt able to. But the Ridgeways were well-known in Honolulu, and she had felt obliged to go, if only to scotch any rumours which might be circulating about Jason and Ellen Ridgeway.

And, it was Ellen Ridgeway herself who confirmed her worst suspicions. In a tearful voice, she had confessed that Jeff must have found out about her and Jason, and that she would never forgive herself for what she had made him do.

Jason had come upon them then, and Laura had known he was furious at her intervention. In spite of the fact that she had arrived in the powerful little sports car he had bought her to go shopping, he insisted on her driving home with him, and it was in the back of one of his luxurious limousines that they had had their last confrontation.

In trembling tones, Laura had told him exactly what Ellen Ridgeway had said, and far from denying it, Jason had turned on her instead. 'You don't trust me, do you?' he had demanded. 'You never have, and I guess you never will.'

'That's not true...'

'What is true then? That you didn't believe I was in San Francisco? That you came to the Colony Room spying on me?'

'No...' Laura caught her breath. 'I was invited to a party! I didn't know you might be there. And—and you weren't in San Francisco, were you?'

'I told you I couldn't explain right then.'

'But you never have, have you? You...you've changed. You don't talk to me any more. And...and since Jeff Ridgeway...since he...'

'Killed himself?' put in Jason callously. 'Why don't you say it? Yes? Since Ridgeway took his own life— what? I've been spending time with his widow?'

Laura moistened her lips. 'Have you?'

'Why should I tell you? If I was to suggest that Ellen lied to you, you wouldn't believe me, so why should I give myself the hassle? So far as Ridgeway's death is concerned—I admit it, I was involved. But I don't regret it!'

Laura eventually left that night, while Jason was downstairs in the club, a guest at a dinner party she had refused to attend. He had left after another painful exchange, and Laura had been pacing about the apartment, undecided what she should do, when Regina called.

Jason's ex-wife had asked to speak to her husband first, and Laura had had to explain that he was not available. It hadn't been easy admitting that they were spending the evening apart, and Regina was quick to make the connection.

'I did wonder if you might still be there,' she remarked maliciously. 'If what I hear is right, my dear ex-husband is running true to form.'

'I don't know what you mean.'

Laura had tried to feign innocence, but Regina had heard the catch in her voice, and she was unforgiving. 'The new woman in Jason's life,' she declared mockingly. 'Do not pretend you do not know about her. It is common knowledge that he has been spending a great deal of time in company with the Ridgeways, and even you cannot believe that it was Jeffrey who sustained his interest for so long.'

There was more of the same dates and places when they had been seen together, which Laura could not refute. And although she had known from the beginning Regina would do anything she could to split them up, she was hurting too much to analyse how much of what the woman said was true. She needed to get away, as far away from Jason as possible, she thought, to get things into perspective. And if Regina's call had precipitated her flight it was no less necessary in the circumstances.

It had been a comparatively simple matter to leave the island. Taking only one suitcase, she had slipped out of the side entrance of the building and hailed a cab, without anyone seeing her. The overnight flight to Los Angeles had connected with a morning flight to London, and she hadn't really stopped to think until she had stopped running.

Now, she pushed these thoughts aside with an aching heart. In spite of everything, she still couldn't think of Jason without feeling that insistent need inside her. Physically, he disturbed her as much now as he had ever done, and it was useless to deny it. She wanted him. She yearned for the hard strength of his body possessing hers, and no matter how rationally she catalogued his faults when she was awake, at night her emotions governed her brain...

A sudden cessation of sound brought her up on her elbows. Unaware, she had been listening to the sound of running water for some time, but now it had stopped, and her brow furrowed as she looked about the room. She didn't remember the maid coming in and asking her if she wanted a bath, and her pulses quickened instinctively at the automatic connotation. Without hesitating, she thrust her feet out of bed, pausing only a moment when a wave of dizziness swept over her. Too many daiquiris, she thought impatiently, snatching up the satin négligée that matched her nightgown and wrapping it around her. Then, her feet slowing as she reached the dressing room, she approached the bathroom door, turning the handle tentatively and holding her breath as she propelled it inward.

'Did I wake you?' inquired a wry voice at her shoulder, and Laura almost jumped out of her skin. Just as her eyes were registering that—although one of the tubs was three-quarters filled with water—the bathroom was unoccupied, her ears were assaulted by that deep familiar tone. Swinging round, she found Jason right behind her, naked save for the towel wrapped loosely about his hips, and for a moment she was unable to control her emotional reaction.

'I—why—oh, *God*! It was you!' she breathed, remembering her dreams of hallucinating, her hands stretching out to touch the fine hair that filmed his chest, and Jason's lips twisted.

'Yes, it was me,' he conceded roughly, before his hands reached for her, and as he jerked her close against his lean taut body, he added, 'If I'd known my absence would have this kind of effect, I'd have taken a chance and come back sooner.'

The harshness of his words was more than compensated by the hungry pressure of his mouth. Besides, for the moment, Laura was too absorbed with allaying her own tortured senses, and even the thickness of the towel about his hips was too great a barrier between them. With her arms about his waist it was a simple matter to slide her fingers down the hollow of his spine, invading the cream towelling and loosening its knot. When it fell to the floor, she moved sensuously against him, and the powerful thrust of his manhood surged eagerly against her.

'You want me,' he muttered, threading his hands through the silken curtain of her hair. 'Say it! Say it! I want you to admit it.'

'I want you,' she acknowledged breathlessly, hardly aware of what she was saying, and with a sound of satisfaction, Jason swung her into his arms and carried her back into the bedroom...

Some time later, Laura opened her eyes to find Jason propped on one elbow looking down at her, and immediately the realisation of what she had done swept over her. Once again, she had allowed her senses to rule her reason, and this time Jason could be in no doubt that she had initiated their passionate lovemaking.

'Do you know—I believe you've put on a little weight since you came here,' he remarked, running a possessive hand along the curve of her hip and down over her belly.

'Dare I say it suits you?'

'Don't!' With a jack-knifing movement, Laura thrust his hand away and jerked upright, feeling the sweat break out on her forehead when the room revolved as before. 'I...I...have to talk to you. But not now. Lucy will be wondering where I am.'

'I should think Lucy has a pretty good idea,' retorted Jason softly, coming up beside her and allowing his teeth to skim lightly over her shoulder. 'Surely she's told you how delighted she is that we're back together again.'

'We...we're not back together,' said Laura desperately, wiping the back of her hand across her forehead. 'This was a mistake. You frightened me, and...and I lost control.'

'You did, didn't you?' murmured Jason teasingly, taking the lobe of her ear between his teeth and biting it. 'But it was no mistake. So stop trying to pretend it was.'

Laura breathed unsteadily. 'I must get dressed...'

'Why must you?'

'Pam—Pam usually comes over in the mornings,' she stammered huskily, finding it difficult to separate thoughts of her sister from the unwelcome memories she had been nurturing earlier. 'She...she...'

'To hell with Pam!' Jason's hands slid beneath her arms to cup the swollen fullness of her breasts. 'See...' he said thickly, his thumbs probing the thrusting nipples. 'You like this just as much as I do.'

'Jason *don't*!' With a supreme effort, Laura forced

herself away from him, scrambling on to her knees and groping for her satin wrapper. 'You...you don't understand. We have to talk about Mike Kazantis. Why didn't you tell me he and Irene were separated? Why did you tell me he was in Italy, when you knew exactly where he was living? Why did you lie to me? Why did you lie to Pam?'

Jason's lean face took on a look of resignation. 'Lucy told you,' he said flatly. 'It figures.'

'Did you think she wouldn't?'

'No.' He lounged back against the pillows and folded his arms beneath his head. 'You had to know sooner or later. I guess she did me a favour.'

Laura gazed at him. 'You mean—you don't deny it?'

'Deny what? That Mike and Irene are separated? That would be pretty stupid, wouldn't it?'

Laura dragged her robe about her. 'I don't believe this. You deliberately misled me. Why? Why?'

'I didn't want you going and seeing Kazantis,' replied Jason evenly. 'You don't know what kind of man he is. I do.'

Laura gasped. 'And you feel yourself fit to judge him!'

'I do.' Jason regarded her steadily. 'What does your sister say?'

'Pam?' Laura looked blank. 'I haven't discussed this with her!'

'Why not?'

'Why not?' Laura shook her head. 'I—I suppose because I wanted to speak to you first. I couldn't believe you'd do this to us.'

'Do what?' Jason's patience was thinning. 'Grow up, Laura. He's still not free, is he? And Pamela was quite willing to make alternative arrangements.'

Laura's lips parted. 'Pam? But she doesn't even know he's married.'

'Doesn't she?'

'You said you hadn't told her.'

'No.' Jason's hands fell to his sides. 'As I recall it, we never did get to finish our conversation about your sister, did we?'

'But…what are you saying?'

'Nothing too obscure.' Jason shrugged. 'Simply that your sister knew the score right from day one.'

'You mean with Mike?' Laura was appalled.

'No. I mean with me,' corrected Jason shortly. 'I guess she suspected I didn't buy that story about her trying to take her own life.'

'You would know about that,' put in Laura bitterly, and Jason's eyes hardened.

'You really are naïve, aren't you?' he said scornfully. 'Didn't you ever wonder how you could fly five thousand miles and yet still get there in time to save her life?'

Laura moistened her lips. 'I…I assumed she had waited.'

'Oh, she waited all right. A good ten hours in my estimation.'

Laura wouldn't believe it. 'I—I could have missed the flight. The plane could have crashed!'

'But it didn't, did it? I guess she thought it was worth the risk.'

Laura trembled. 'But if you knew this, why did you help her?'

'You know why.'

'To—to force me to come back to you?'

'Means and ends,' said Jason harshly. 'We all live by them.'

'I don't believe this!'

'Why not?' Jason pushed himself into a sitting position, crossing his legs. 'Haven't you always known I've not been exactly sane where you're concerned?'

Laura shook her head. 'Are you telling me there was never any cause for concern where Pam was concerned?'

'No, I'm not saying that.' Jason spoke tolerantly. 'Obviously, when she took the overdose, she was pretty desperate. As I suspected, Kazantis took off as soon as he discovered she was pregnant, and your sister knew she was in trouble. Apparently she didn't have the money for an abortion, even if she'd wanted one, and telephoning you was her last resort. She had some idea that if you came and spoke with Mike you might be able to persuade him to accept his responsibilities.' He grimaced. 'Some chance!'

Laura stared at him with a growing sense of disorientation. 'So…so you decided to use the situation to your own advantage.'

'It wasn't quite like that.' Jason expelled his breath heavily. 'Remember, when you took off for London, I had only your story to go on. It wasn't until I'd spoken to your sister that I got the whole picture.'

'You lied to me!'

'I…embroidered the truth.'

'What do you mean? Mike was never in Italy.'

'He could have been. He does have relatives there, you know.'

Laura hunched her shoulders. 'What a fool I've been!'

'Oh, Christ!' With an oath, Jason vaulted over the bed to her side. 'You haven't been a fool. You've acted in what you thought were your sister's best interests, and in so doing given yourself time to realise that what we had is still as powerful as it ever was.' His hand tipped her resisting face towards him. 'Dear God, haven't we wasted enough time? Don't make me wait another three years to tell me you still care!'

His voice was persuasive, his hand gentle against her soft skin, the taut strength of his body shameless in its beauty...but Laura knew she could not believe him. Nothing had changed. He was still the man who thought he could do no wrong, and even if she could forgive him his infidelity, she could not forgive him for causing another man to take his own life.

With a moan of anguish, she tore herself away from him, scrambling off the bed and backing up until her shoulders touched the wall behind her. 'Don't!' she said. 'Don't ever touch me again! Just call your pilot. Have him fly me back to Oahu. I'm going back to London, and if you try to stop me, I may just follow Pamela's example!'

CHAPTER TWELVE

LAURA HAD BEEN back in London three weeks when she had an unexpected visitor.

She was staying in Pierce's house. He had insisted she do nothing about finding a place of her own until she had had time to think about what she wanted to do, and Laura had accepted his dictates simply because she didn't have the strength to argue. Besides, she knew he had not given up hope of persuading her to make her home with him permanently; and with a trip to the Far East coming up, it did not seem practical to take on the expense of a flat until her return.

Pierce had asked remarkably few questions about her sudden change of plans, although he had been surprised to learn that Pamela was staying on in Hawaii. 'I'd have thought she'd want to be with her sister at a time like this,' he commented, when Laura let it be known that she was not returning to England. 'Oh, well…I suppose she's old enough to look after herself. You never know, she may persuade your erstwhile employer to marry her.'

This was something Laura could not discuss, but as luck would have it, the 'phone rang at that moment and the painful moment passed. Eventually, she would be able to view that possibility with equanimity, Laura told herself, but for the present it was too raw and vulnerable to expose.

Leaving Kaulanai had been the most difficult thing she had ever done in her life. When she had run from Jason before, it had been with the memory of his anger

185

ringing in her ears, and the knowledge that he had already replaced her with Ellen Ridgeway. This time, it was different. This time, he had asked her to stay and when she had refused, he had shut himself away in his study, so that she had not seen him again before Jonah drove her to the airport.

Of course, Lucy had begged her not to go. She had been quite tearful when she said her goodbyes, and Laura's suggestion that she might visit her in London had not met with any enthusiasm. 'Daddy cares about you,' she exclaimed tremulously, cupping her neck with nervous fingers. 'Please, Laura, give him another chance!'

Pamela was surprised, but not disappointed. 'I said it was unnecessary for you to stay here,' she commented, when Laura told her she was leaving. 'What's happened? Have you and Jason fallen out? I had the feeling something was wrong, when he stayed away so long.'

'It's a personal matter,' Laura had responded tensely, not prepared to bare her feelings to anyone. 'It might have been easier if you had been honest with me. Jason tells me you knew Mike was married all along.'

'He was a louse!' said Pamela succinctly, showing no particular malice. 'But you've no idea how I felt—thousands of miles from anyone who cared about me, and Mrs Goldstein threatening to fire me if I was late again.' She shook her head. 'I felt so sick in the mornings—so dizzy! Sometimes I really wanted to die!'

Laura had had cause to remember that particular statement since she came back to England. Several mornings lately she had developed a feeling of nausea when she got out of bed, and the bitter irony of her condition did not make accepting it any easier. She was pregnant. She was sure of it. But unlike Pamela, she had nowhere to turn for help.

She did think about telling Pierce, but she was half afraid of his reaction. Knowing him as she did, she was almost sure he would insist on her either informing Jason of his responsibilities, or marrying himself without delay. Neither alternative had any merit so far as Laura was concerned. To tell Jason he was to be a father for a second time might have certain selfish advantages, but she would not blackmail him into marrying her, even if she could. And as for marrying Pierce—well, she simply couldn't see herself marrying anyone other than her child's father for, whatever his sins, he was the only man she would ever love. She might not respect him; she might not even *like* him; but feeling as she did, she could not share her life with another man.

May had given way to June, and the days were getting longer. Since Laura's return, the weather had been unseasonably chilly, but one morning she awakened to find blue skies and rising temperatures. Summer had at last arrived, and she got out of bed with a determined sense of optimism. She couldn't go on living in a vacuum, she told herself firmly. Today, she would tell Pierce about the baby, and explain to him her reasons for keeping it to herself.

Her recovering spirits received something of a setback, when nausea sent her hurrying into the bathroom. Resting her damp forehead against the cool glaze of the mirror, she acknowledged it would take more than a sunny day to solve her problems, but whatever happened, she was going to keep Jason's child.

At breakfast, Pierce was absorbed with opening his mail, and sipping her unsweetened tea—she could no longer face coffee in the mornings—Laura had no opportunity to broach the subject closest to her heart. However, when the meal was over, Pierce suggested attending to the letters he had to write straight away, and Laura followed him into his study with a sense of anticipation.

'It's such a lovely day, I thought we might go out after lunch,' Pierce remarked, seating himself behind his desk. 'How does a trip to Bournemouth appeal to you? A breath of sea air, and a walk along the promenade. Exactly the kind of outing to put some colour into your cheeks. You're looking pale, Laura. I've noticed it for some time. Even your tan is fading, and we can't have that, now can we?'

Laura pressed the palms of her hands together, and taking her chance, she said carefully, 'As a matter of fact, Pierce, I did want to talk to you about that.'

'About what?' Pierce was re-reading a letter that had arrived that morning, and was only half listening to her.

'About—about my not feeling well,' murmured Laura awkwardly, and he lifted his head to fix her with a concerned stare.

'You're not ill, are you?' he exclaimed. His expression deepened to one of anxiety. 'That's not why you came back to England, is it?'

'No. No.' Laura moistened her upper lip. 'I'm not ill...' and as she sought for words to break it to him gently, they heard the doorbell chime.

Pierce's head lifted. 'Visitors?' he said impatiently. 'At this hour?' He pulled out his pocket watch, flipped open the lid and looked at it. 'How inconvenient!'

Until Mrs Barnes, Pierce's housekeeper, had informed them who it was, Laura could say no more, and she stifled her impatience as the minutes stretched.

The knock on the door, when it came, was almost an anti-climax, and Pierce viewed the buxom figure of his housekeeper with some frustration. 'Not now, Mrs Barnes,' he said. 'Whoever it is, tell them I'm tied up at the moment. Nine forty-five in the morning is far too early for interviews.'

'It's not someone for you, Mr Carver,' Mrs Barnes informed him stiffly. 'It's a lady to see Miss Huyton. I told her you were working, and that you didn't like to be disturbed, but the lady was more insistent. She says she's come all the way from America, and it's a matter of some urgency.'

'Pamela!' exclaimed Laura immediately, springing to her feet. 'Oh, Pierce, I'm sorry about this, but if Pam's come all this way to see me, it must be something important.'

'The lady said her name was Mrs…Kazandis, miss,' put in the housekeeper uncertainly. 'Would that be your sister?'

'Kazan*tis*?' corrected Laura automatically, stopping in her tracks. 'Mrs Kazantis? But—that must be…'

'Me!' said a tentative voice from behind Mrs Barnes, and Laura's eyes widened at the astonishing appearance of Jason's sister.

'Irene!' she said faintly. And then, with increasing urgency: 'Is something wrong? Has something happened to Jason? Oh, God!' Her head swam. 'It is Jason, isn't it? You wouldn't have come here otherwise. What's happened to him? Is he ill? Has there been an accident? Tell me! Tell me!'

'Laura, calm down!' Irene came instantly into the study, brushing past the stunned figure of the housekeeper and giving Pierce an appealing look. 'I came to talk to you, that's all.' She put an arm about Laura's trembling shoulders. 'I came straight from the airport. Now…stop getting yourself in a state, and I'll explain.'

Laura gazed at her with anxious eyes. 'Jason's all right? You swear?'

'Of course.' Irene looked helplessly at Pierce. 'I'm sorry about this. I didn't mean to upset anyone.'

'But you evidently have,' remarked Pierce drily, recovering from his own shock at Laura's reaction. He turned to the housekeeper. 'That will do, Mrs Barnes. We'll call you if we need you.'

'Yes, sir.'

The housekeeper departed with some reluctance, and after she had gone, Pierce came towards the two women, holding out his hand. 'Pierce Carver, Mrs Kazantis,' he introduced himself politely. 'I assume you must be another member of the family.'

'I'm Jason's sister,' said Irene ruefully, returning his greeting. 'I got to know Laura about four years ago. When she and Jason were together.'

'Together?'

Pierce arched one narrow eyebrow, and Laura expelled her breath on a sigh. 'Jason and I lived together for almost two years,' she admitted quietly. 'I was only his secretary for a few months. After that, I...'

'...shared more than his confidence,' finished Pierce ironically. 'Yes.' He shrugged. 'That doesn't exactly come as a surprise to me.'

Laura lifted her head. 'It doesn't?'

'I am not completely unworldly, my dear,' he responded. 'And I would have had to be totally insensitive not to comprehend the tension between you and Montefiore that night at my club. I suspected you had had a relationship. I hoped that it was over.'

'It was!' Laura gave Irene a doubtful look. 'It is!'

'Could I talk to Laura alone, do you think, Mr Carver?' inquired Irene smoothly. 'I do want to talk to her about Jason, and I'd prefer it if we could speak privately.'

'Why not?' Pierce's nostrils flared. 'I shall be in the library, if you want me, Laura. Mrs Kazantis.' He bowed his head, and moving with his loose-limbed stride, he left the room.

Alone with Jason's sister, Laura was at a loss for words. She couldn't imagine why Irene had come here, and she was still suffering from the shock her appearance had given her. If Jason had had something to say to her, why couldn't he have come himself? she wondered unsteadily. Now that Irene had reassured her that he was not ill or injured, her indignation at his continued interference in her life flowered anew. Why couldn't he just leave her alone? It was hard enough, carrying his child inside her, and knowing she could never share it with him.

'Your Mr Carver evidently thinks a lot about you,' said Irene suddenly, breaking the silence that had fallen since the door had closed behind him, and Laura bent her head.

'He's a good friend.'

'He'd like to be a lot more than that, in my opinion,' remarked Irene drily. 'Are you in love with him?'

'In love with Pierce?' Laura gazed at her blankly. 'Of course I'm not in love with Pierce. We don't have that kind of a relationship.'

'So why did you leave Jason?'

Laura's face suffused with colour. 'I beg your pardon?'

'Laura, please…' Irene propped herself on the edge of Pierce's desk and regarded the younger girl with troubled eyes. She was like Jason, Laura thought, her heart twisting at the realisation. Slim and dark and attractive, but without his height or muscular build. 'We have to be honest with one another. I didn't fly all this way just to say hello.'

Laura's tongue circled her lips. 'Why did you fly all this way then? Did Jason send you?'

'Jason!' Irene rolled her eyes expressively. 'If my brother knew I was here, he'd be furious. But—well—my mother begged me to come, and I have to say, I'm concerned about him myself.'

'About who?' Laura swallowed. 'About Jason?' Her pulse quickened. 'But…you said he was all right. You said…'

'I know what I said.' Irene interrupted her, before she could work herself into a state again. 'And he's not—ill, exactly…'

'What does that mean?'

'It means what it says.' Irene gestured to a chair. 'Why don't you sit down, Laura. You look as if you need to. Really, I'll tell you everything, but you must stop jumping to conclusions.

Laura shook her head and remained standing, and with a grimace, Irene continued. 'Look,' she said, 'I get the feeling that in spite of everything that's happened, you *do* care what happens to that stubborn brother of mine. So why are you here in London, while he's trying to kill himself out in Hawaii?'

Laura blanched. 'Trying to *kill* himself?'

'A figure of speech.' Irene sighed. 'But that's what he's going to do if he doesn't pull himself together.'

'I don't understand.'

'Sure, you do. You walked out on him, didn't you? For the *second* time!'

Laura twisted her hands together. 'You obviously don't know the whole story…'

'Oh, I know the story all right.' Irene gazed at her impatiently. 'And in spite of what Jason promised my father, I'm going to tell you the truth.'

Laura shook her head. 'Irene…'

'Listen to me.' Irene would not be silenced. 'I know you left Jason because he told you he was implicated in Jeff Ridgeway's death, but he never told you what Ridgeway had done to our father!'

Laura blinked. 'Your father?'

'Yes.' Irene raked impatient fingers through her cap of dark hair. 'It's a complicated story, but I'll try and make it brief.' She paused, and then went on: 'A lot of years ago, my father got in trouble with the law. I hate to tell you this, but it had to do with drugs, and he was arrested. Well, he was not without influence, and he succeeded, with the help of Regina's father, to shake the charge.'

Laura gazed at her. 'When was this?'

'I've told you. A lot of years ago.'

'How many years?'

'Eighteen, maybe. Nineteen, what does it matter?'

Laura took a breath. 'About the time Jason married Regina?'

'About that time, I guess.' Irene frowned. 'Oh, yes. I see Jason's told you about that. I didn't realise.'

'Jason didn't,' said Laura heavily. 'Someone else did. Please—go on.'

'Okay.' Irene tugged at her ear lobe. 'Where was I?'

'You'd just told me your father wasn't convicted.'

'That's right.' Irene nodded. 'Okay. So we come to Jeff Ridgeway. I guess you would call him a—speculator.'

'He was in business, wasn't he?'

'In a manner of speaking.' Irene bit her lip. 'Somehow—don't ask me how—he'd found out about my father. Unknown to any of us, he'd been blackmailing my father for years, using the money to buy up small businesses that were in financial difficulties, taking over people's lives with as much compassion as he had shown my father. Oh...' she made a dismissive gesture, 'I'm not saying my father didn't deserve to be punished for what he'd done. He was guilty, and he should have gone to prison. Jason had no sympathy for him, believe me, and if it hadn't been for my mother, he'd never have allowed himself to be used like that. But...he did, and I guess he thought it was over. We all did. Until Jason became involved.'

Laura's throat felt dry. 'Are you saying that when Jason found out, he chose to punish Ridgeway by seducing his wife?'

'That little...' Irene bit off an epithet. 'Hell, no. Jason wasn't interested in Ellen Ridgeway.'

'Then why...'

'Let me finish.' Irene walked round Pierce's desk and flopped down into his deep leather armchair. 'Perhaps I should tell you: when Ridgeway decided to shift his operations to the islands, he assumed he could use Jason in much the same way as he had used my father.'

'You mean...he tried to blackmail Jason?' Laura was horrified.

'He tried,' said Irene flatly. 'But Jason is not like my father.'

Laura's brow furrowed. 'But what could he do?'

Irene hesitated. 'I suppose you could say, he took the law into his own hands.'

Laura pressed her hands to her stomach. 'He didn't...he didn't *push* Ridgeway off the balcony?'

'No.' Irene's lips twisted. 'I guess the man took his

own life, although there was speculation afterwards that it might have been accidental. These things do happen, though not usually so conveniently.'

Laura nodded. 'Go on.'

'Well...' Irene considered her words, 'when Jason was approached, he decided to make some inquiries of his own. There's a firm of inquiry agents he sometimes employs—'

'I know.' Laura quivered.

'—and he put them on the job. It took some time— almost eighteen months, I believe—but eventually they came up with something that gave Jason the weapon he needed. Somewhere along the line, Ridgeway had discovered the quick profits that could be made from drugs himself, and although Jason had no actual proof, he knew enough to take a chance and go for it.'

'How?' Laura was confused. 'Surely if Jason got involved with drugs, he was playing into the man's hands.'

'He would have, if that's what he'd done.' Irene nodded. 'He also knew he hadn't a cat in hell's chance of getting the man convicted. Ridgeway took no chances— but that's where Ellen came in.'

Laura stiffened. 'Jason did get involved with her then?'

'He *used* her. He let her think he was interested in her, until she was willing to go to any lengths to have him.'

'Oh, Irene...'

'Don't you believe me?' Irene shook her head. 'Laura, I know my brother. I know he's no angel. But if he says he had nothing to do with Ellen Ridgeway, then you'd better believe him.'

'He didn't say that,' said Laura tensely. 'All he said was that I didn't trust him.'

'Well, you didn't, did you?' said Irene practically. 'You don't even believe me.'

'I don't know what to believe any more.' Laura put a hand to her head. 'I thought Jeff Ridgeway killed himself because of Jason's affair with his wife.'

'Yes. Well…I somehow think it would take more than his wife's infidelity to shake our victim,' remarked Irene flatly. 'She was hardly irreplaceable. She was his third wife.'

'She was?'

'Didn't you know?'

'How could I?'

'Hmm.' Irene shrugged. 'Still, I digress. Where was I? Oh, yes, you're still wondering how Jason got to him.' She uttered a short mirthless laugh. 'My brother has friends in strange places. Using his influence, he managed to find out when a consignment of heroin was coming in, and arrange for it to be stolen.'

'Stolen?'

'Don't look so shocked. It was only stolen so that Ridgeway would be forced to tell the men who paid him, it was gone. Then, later, after Jason had learned of Ridgeway's whereabouts from Ellen, it was hidden in the Ridgeway complex.'

'But why?' Laura was bewildered. 'What good was that?'

'Can you imagine what Ridgeway's paymasters would think when they found the stuff hidden on his premises?'

'But how would they know?'

'Think about it.'

'Jason…told them.'

'Someone did.'

Laura sank down weakly into her chair. 'I can't take this in.'

'No. It's not a pleasant story, is it?'

'Then why didn't he tell me?' Laura shook her head. 'If he'd only told me...'

'How could he?' Irene looked at her steadily. 'You were not his wife. You were free to walk out at any time—as you did. How could he put his father's life in your hands?'

Laura swallowed. 'But...you've told me.'

'Because someone had to. Laura, Jason loves you. Can't you believe that? My God, do you think either my mother or I would put our whole family at risk, if we didn't believe he cared.'

'And...and what about me?'

'You?' Irene lay back wearily in the chair. 'Your feelings, I think, are not in doubt. I guess I knew that the minute I walked in here, and you almost had hysterics because you thought Jason had been hurt.'

CHAPTER THIRTEEN

LAURA SPENT the night with Jason's parents in San Francisco, and flew on to Oahu the following day. The afternoon flight from the Bay City was delayed, however, and it was early evening before the big jet landed in Honolulu. Once again, Laura had to run the gamut of the holidaymakers who were flocking to the islands, and she was grateful for the chauffeur-driven hire car Jason's father had arranged to pick her up at the airport.

She asked the driver to take her first to the Ilikai, the famous hotel by the yacht harbour where Jason kept a suite of rooms at his disposal. Irene had told her that Jason had left Kaulanai the same day she did, and since then he had been virtually inaccessible. The only person who had had any conversation with him was Lucas Kamala, and it was he who had informed Jason's mother of her son's declining mental state.

'Luke says he's been drinking more than is good for him, and he's hardly eating a thing,' Irene explained, on the flight from London to San Francisco. 'I tried to speak to him on the 'phone, and my father actually went to the club to try and reach him, but he wasn't available—or said he wasn't! Whatever you do, Laura, don't let him turn you away. He needs you. He wants you. But he's just stubborn enough to imagine you've come to him out of pity.'

'Pity!' Laura had gazed unseeingly out of the window of the plane, wishing she had had the faith to ignore what Ellen Ridgeway had said and believe him. 'He may

198

never forgive me,' she murmured, speaking barely audibly, but Irene heard her and squeezed her hand.

'You've got to make him. For all our sakes,' she said fiercely. 'Remember—my father blames himself for everything that's happened.'

In the car, driving to the Ilikai, Laura wondered, a little cynically, whether Marco Montefiore might not be more concerned with saving his own soul, rather than that of his son. Jason's mother seemed genuinely concerned, but his father had used him once, and was perhaps not above using Laura, too. For the first time, she understood why Jason had so little respect for the man who had sired him, and it made her all the more determined to convince him that she cared.

It was odd, she thought, how Pamela's reckless actions had given her this second chance. Without her sister's involvement with Mike Kazantis, she might never have seen Jason again. She might even have married Pierce one day, never knowing that the man she had cared for so deeply was still there in her life, a silent witness to his own betrayal.

The spacious lobby of the Ilikai was full of tourists, checking in and checking out. Porters hove back and forth with trolleys loaded with suitcases and plastic bags, and there was a bustling air of organised chaos. The desk was busy, but Laura managed to attract the attention of a young receptionist, and asked if Mr Montefiore was in the hotel. If the man was surprised that a rather travel-weary young woman was asking for one of his most wealthy clients, he hid it very well, though Laura had to admit to herself that the short-sleeved blue shirt and peg-waisted cotton pants had suffered in the prolonged wait at the airport and the five-hour flight from the mainland.

'Mr Montefiore is not in his suite,' he responded politely, probably relieved that he could be honest, Laura suspected. 'I'm sorry. I don't know when he'll be back. I should try again tomorrow.'

'Thank you.'

Laura accepted her dismissal with good grace, acknowledging that it had been unlikely that Jason would be in his room at nine o'clock at night. She could only pray now that he might be at the Blue Orchid Club. The idea that he could, conceivably, be finding solace elsewhere, did not bear thinking about.

It was a short distance from the Ilikai to the Blue Orchid, and after getting out of the car, Laura dismissed the driver. If Jason wasn't here, she would have to wait until the morning to reach him, and she could not keep the man hanging about indefinitely, when she could just as easily hail a cab.

Entering the club, in such casual attire and with her suitcase in her hand, Laura felt horribly conspicuous. It was three years since she had last been here, and although she knew Jason had said Lucas Kamala was in charge, she saw no one she recognised as she crossed the veined marble lobby.

'Can I help you?'

She had known there was no chance of her reaching the lift without being apprehended, and now she turned to face the man who had spoken with determined brightness. 'I...er...I'm looking for Mr Kamala,' she began, deciding she might have more success if she spoke to Jason's assistant, and then her lips parted in surprise as she recognised the man who had addressed her. 'Phil' she exclaimed. 'Phil Logan!' She admired his white dinner jacket and neatly-creased trousers. 'I didn't realise it was you.'

The man, who had worked in the club bar when Laura

had last seen him, gazed at her in disbelief. 'As I live and breathe!' he exclaimed. 'What are you doing here? I thought Jason said you had gone back to England.'

'I had. I did.' Laura glanced nervously towards the lifts. 'I...I'm looking for Luke. Is he upstairs?'

'Yes.' Phil regarded her doubtfully. 'But he's not alone Jason's here, you know.'

Laura's breath escaped in a fluttery sigh. 'He is?'

'Sure.' Phil hesitated. 'If you like, I can ask Luke to come down here. I guess you don't want to see Jason. As I hear it, you and he are all washed up.'

Laura's eyes darted to his. 'Who told you that?'

'I don't know. Luke, I guess.' He paused. 'You want me to ring him?'

'*No!* That is...' Laura swallowed to ease her parched throat. 'Could I just go up, do you think? I...would like to see Jason, too.'

Phil frowned. 'Look...it's none of my business, I know, and Jason bawled me out the last time when you rang the club, and I wouldn't give you his number. But—well, I don't think it's a good idea for you to go up there right now. Let me ring Luke. He'll put you in the picture.'

'Jason's sister's already put me in the picture,' said Laura quietly. 'Phil, let me go up. I have to see Jason, so it might as well be now, hmm?'

He let her go with some misgivings, offering to take charge of her suitcase until she came back. But, as the metal cylinder made its speedy ascent to the penthouse floor, Laura guessed he would not be able to contain his uncertainty, and she was not really surprised when Lucas Kamala was waiting for the lift doors to open.

'Long time, no see, Laura,' he said gently, his drawling island tones almost reducing her to tears. 'Phil had to let me know you were coming. Don't be too mad with him. He's only doing his job.'

'Oh, Lucas!' Laura stepped back from his embrace and scraped the back of her hand across her cheeks. 'I have to see Jason. Irene told me he won't talk to anyone, but he's got to talk to me.'

Lucas regarded her compassionately, but his words were less sympathetic. 'I'm not sure that would solve anything, Laura,' he said frankly. 'Seeing you again is not going to change the situation. I think perhaps you should have stayed away.'

Laura gasped. 'But why?'

'You know why.' Lucas spread his hands. 'When you walked out on him three years ago, he took it badly. For months, he lived the life of a recluse. Why do you think he got out of this apartment? Because it held too many memories of when you were together!'

Laura stared at him. 'I didn't know…'

'How could you?' Lucas shook his head. 'Then—a couple of months ago, Jason told us you were coming back. I didn't hear the details until later, but it seems you had asked him for his help with your sister, and we all thought you were back for good. When you left again, I tell you, Jason really went to pieces.'

Laura trembled. 'But he's here, isn't he?'

'Yes.' Lucas acknowledged the fact with some reluctance.

'So let me see him.'

'You can't. At least…not right away.'

'Why not?' Laura was defensive. 'Lucas, I can't tell you the whole story right now, but I'm not about to walk out on Jason again.'

Lucas expelled his breath heavily. 'How can I believe that?'

'You just have to.' Laura held up her head. 'Lucas, I haven't flown all this way, just to be turned away by…by someone else. If Jason doesn't want me, let him tell me so himself.'

'He can't. Not now.' Lucas glanced uneasily along the carpeted corridor which led to the penthouse suite. 'Laura, let me talk to him first. Let me tell him you're here. If you haven't already checked in to a hotel, do so. I'll 'phone you as soon as I've spoken to him, I promise.'

'No.' Laura stood her ground. She was very much afraid that if she left here—if she allowed Lucas to speak to Jason first—she would get no further than his father had. She had to stand firm. It was her only chance.

'Laura, please…'

Lucas put his hand on her arm, but when she realised he was trying to urge her back into the lift, she pulled away from him. 'No,' she said unsteadily. 'No, I won't let you do this!' and before he could prevent her, she ran off along the corridor.

She heard him following her, but Lucas was not as young as he used to be, and too many business lunches and the wine he had consumed with them, slowed him down. Besides, she knew the layout of the penthouse floor as well as he did, and the door to what had been Jason's apartment was standing ajar. Rushing through it, she half expected to find Jason in the living room, but although the lamps were lit, the room was empty.

She halted uncertainly, and the few seconds she took to survey her surroundings gave Lucas a chance to catch up. 'Laura, this isn't very sensible,' he panted, stomping into the apartment behind her, and when his eyes swung warily across the room, Laura guessed where Jason must be.

Without giving him a chance to catch his breath, she strode swiftly through the door which she knew from past experience led to the bedrooms. Unhesitatingly, she paused before the room she and Jason used to share, and then, with trembling fingers, pushed the door open.

As she had suspected, Jason was lying on the bed. In the light from the hall behind her, she perceived he was still dressed, however, though he had shed his jacket and his shirt was unbuttoned. His eyes were closed when the door was opened, but the intruding light caused him to shift restlessly in its illumination, and he muttered indistinctly, 'For Christ's sake, Luke—you're blinding me!'

But Luke was not there. When Laura automatically glanced behind her, she saw that Jason's assistant had not followed her. She was on her own—alone with a man who hadn't yet identified her, and who was evidently somewhat the worse for alcohol. There was a half empty bottle of Scotch on the table beside the bed, and the sweet-sour smell of strong liquor pervading the atmosphere.

There was a lamp by the door, and before shutting out the light and losing all knowledge of her whereabouts, Laura bent down and turned it on, flooding the room with a warm amber radiance. Then, as Jason groaned and rolled away from the glow, she closed the door and advanced towards the bed.

'Jason,' she ventured tentatively. 'Jason, it's not Luke, it's me—Laura.'

Jason moved then, a sudden twisting movement that brought him up against the pillows, to gaze at her with wary eyes. 'Laura?' he echoed harshly. 'My God! Am I hallucinating?'

'You're not hallucinating. It's really me,' said Laura

huskily, trying to hide her dismay at his appearance. At least two days' growth of beard was bristling on his chin, and his pale eyes were red-rimmed and bloodshot. He looked ill—ill and gaunt; and her heart twisted painfully at the knowledge that she had played some part in his condition. 'I—just arrived a little over an hour ago. I went to the Ilikai, but of course you weren't there…'

'How did you get in?' Jason was recovering from the shock of seeing her, and his voice had perceptibly hardened. 'I told Luke. He knew…'

'He tried to stop me,' Laura put in hurriedly, 'but I wouldn't let him. I have to talk to you, Jason. Please, can I—'

'We've got nothing to talk about,' he retorted bleakly. Then, raking back the tumbled hair from his forehead, he reached for the bottle beside the bed. 'I want you to go—now; this minute. We've got nothing to say to one another, and you're just wasting my time.'

'Your drinking time, you mean?' demanded Laura unsteadily. 'I wouldn't have thought it of you, Jason. I thought you had more—*guts* than that!'

'What would you know about it?' he inquired grimly, raising the bottle to his lips. 'What would you know about me? You never knew me; you only thought you did.'

'Obviously.' Laura took a deep breath. 'But for someone who reputedly despises other people's weaknesses, you're not exactly a prime example of self-control, are you?'

'Go away, Laura.' Jason's mouth compressed. 'I don't have to listen to a lecture from you. I'll go to the devil my own way. Keep your moralising for those who need it!'

'Oh, Jason…'

'Oh, Jason—what? Why have you come here, Laura. It's not because you care what happens to me. You made your feelings very clear the last time we spoke together. You want out of our relationship; well, okay—I want it, too!'

'No, you don't!' Laura gave a hopeless little groan, and sank down on to the bed beside him. 'Jason, why didn't you tell me how you really felt? Why did you let me go on thinking you were only using me?'

'I don't know what you're talking about,' said Jason broodingly, gazing down at the bottle in his hand. 'Okay, so when you came back, I thought you wanted to make up. I was soon disabused of that notion, wasn't I? All we seem to do is hurt one another, Laura, and quite frankly I don't care any more what the hell you do!'

'That's not true!'

'It is true.' This close his eyes had a brittle penetration that frightened her by its opacity. 'I don't need you any more, Laura. You were like a fever in my brain, but now I'm exorcising you.' He lifted the bottle. 'That's what this is. The natives used to call it fire water. The heat of this—fire water—is burning you out of my blood!'

'I don't believe you!'

With an impulsive gesture, Laura snatched the bottle out of his hand and flung it away across the room. It shattered against the far wall, and the gurgling sound of leaking alcohol was magnified in the silence that followed.

Then, with uncontrolled fury, Jason swore at her. 'You crazy bitch!' he burst out savagely. 'What are you trying to do to me? Why have you come here? What do you want? Oh, don't tell me—my father sent you. He's scared to death I'm going to follow Ridgeway's example. Well, don't worry. I won't involve you. I won't involve any of you. Just let me live my own life, will you?'

Laura's shoulders sagged. 'Jason...' She had to tell the truth. 'Jason—Irene came to see me...'

'Really?'

'Yes, really.' Laura moistened her lips. 'She...she and your parents are worried about you.'

'I'll be!'

'They are. And...and so was I.' She twisted her hands together. 'Particularly when Irene told me that—that I'd been wrong about you and—and the Ridgeways.'

Jason's lips twisted. 'They must be desperate!'

'They are.' Laura put out her hands towards him, but he shifted so that she could not reach him. 'Jason I'm sorry. I know that's hardly adequate, but I am sorry. If I could undo the past, I would. I was a fool. I should have believed you. But... I...I could see no other reason why a man like Jeff Ridgeway would take his own life. It was naïve perhaps, but not so unlikely, surely. And—and it wasn't as if we were married, was it?'

'Married?' Jason's tone was bitter. 'No. No, I didn't make that mistake a second time. That's one thing in my favour.'

Laura winced. 'Jason, please...'

'Look. Why don't you get out of here, hmm? Okay...it was good of you to come, and I'm sure my family appreciates it, but like you said, you can't undo the past. We had our chance, and we blew it. That's all there is to say.'

Laura got up from the bed. 'So you don't want me,' she said, through stiff lips. 'Irene was wrong.'

Jason's smile was sardonic. 'She surely was,' he drawled mockingly, and the derisive twist to his lips broke Laura's resolve. His anger she could take; his bitterness she deserved; but his deliberate cruelty was more than she could bear.

Backing away from the bed, she made it to the door, fumbling behind her for the handle and wrenching it open. The air in the corridor was infinitely cooler, and less charged, and with a supreme effort she turned and walked back into the living room.

Lucas was there, as she had expected, his face mirroring the anxiety he was feeling. 'That sound,' he said. 'Like breaking glass. What happened? What did you do to him?'

'What did *I* do to *him*?' choked Laura, struggling desperately to hold back her tears. 'Lucas, I…I…'

'She smashed the bottle of Scotch,' said Jason's voice from behind her, and Laura's knees would hardly support her as she turned disbelievingly to face him. 'Sorry about the mess, Luke,' he added coolly, propping his shoulder against the door frame. 'I'll get someone to clean it up. Just get out of here, would you? Laura and I have some things to clear up.'

It was difficult to decide which of them was the most shocked, and Laura saw Luke's mouth sag as the order—for it was nothing less—was issued. 'You want *me* to leave?' he echoed blankly, and Jason massaged his neck muscles as he moved into the room.

'Briefly,' he agreed, and meeting his gaze Laura could glean nothing from it. 'We'll get out of here in fifteen minutes. Just give me time to shave and take a shower.'

'Okay.' Lucas looked at Laura's pale face. 'Are you all right?'

'She's fine,' said Jason, with an edge to his voice, and Lucas shrugged.

'Right. Right, I'm going,' he muttered, shaking his

head. 'I guess I'll see you later.' He grimaced. 'Take your time.'

The minute the door closed, Jason turned back towards the inner hall that led to the bedrooms and bathrooms. 'Take a seat,' he said, for all the world as though Laura was some stranger he was entertaining, and she looked after him weakly, not knowing what to think.

Five minutes of pacing about the living room brought her no nearer a solution, and abandoning her constraint, she went after him. Why was he keeping her here if what he had said was true? Was it only for appearances that he was being civil to her? Was this elaborate façade just a means to deceive his employees?

The shower in the bathroom adjoining the main bedroom was running, and although she knew the most sensible thing to do would be to wait until he was finished, Laura wasn't feeling very sensible right then. Her mind was catapulting from one thought to another, and her body was reacting to the stress she was putting on it. She had to see him; she had to talk to him; she had to know if this was an end, or a beginning.

'Jason...' she said tentatively, stepping into the bathroom and stopping short at the sight of his lean body, twisting and turning beneath the cooling spray. He had left the cubicle door open, and she saw, with a pang, how much weight he had lost since her departure. He was losing it, and she was gaining it, she thought tremulously, running nervous hands over her still-flat stomach, and it was as she was doing this that he became aware of her.

He had shaved, she saw at once, the streaks of blood on his chin evidence of the unsteadiness of his hand, and it was this that made her take one more chance. 'Oh, Jason,' she said distractedly, 'Jason I never stopped loving you!' and he jerked off the tap and came unsteadily towards her.

'You know,' he said, resting his wet arms on her shoulders and looking down into her eyes, 'fire water takes a hell of a time to work its way through your system. I don't think it's had much success so far. I've still got the fever. I guess it's incurable.'

Although Laura protested that Luke might object to their using his bed, Jason wasn't really listening to her. From the moment his arms had closed about her, hauling her slender body close against his muscled frame, he had been barely coherent, and Laura's opposition melted beneath the possession of his hands.

'I'm wet…I know I'm wet,' he muttered, his fingers finding the buttons of her shirt with little consideration for the fact that he was making her wet, too. 'We'll dry one another,' he added, disposing of the remainder of her clothes with the same urgency. 'Oh, God, Laura—I need you!' His mouth sought the parted contours of hers, letting her feel the intimacy of his tongue. 'Why did you leave me?' he grated, the weight of his body an intoxicating stimulant. 'You know that without you, I'm only half alive!'

His lovemaking was intense and passionate, a ravishing assault on her senses, that Laura was more than eager to facilitate. They were hungry for each other, and not until the blissful aftermath of sexual satiation enveloped them, did Jason display a trace of the hostility he had exhibited earlier.

'So now you know,' he said harshly, pushing back the damp tendrils of hair from her forehead with half angry, half tender, fingers. 'I haven't been exactly sane since you left. Are you back to stay, or is this just another flying visit?'

'Do I have to answer that?' Laura cupped his face in her hands, brushing away the lingering smears of blood from his chin with her thumb, and sucking the pad deliberately. 'Jason—I love you. I always have and I always will. And that's something you've never said to me.'

Jason was lying between her legs and now he supported himself on his elbows to look down at her. But when he would have moved, she wound her arms round his neck, and he subsided again with a not uncontented sigh. 'I thought I'd proved how I felt about you,' he said huskily, burying his face between her breasts. 'Over and over and over again. Dear God, there never was another woman, all the time we were together. Do we really need words to make a commitment?'

Laura lifted his head. 'If—if—I hadn't gone away, would you have asked me to marry you?'

Jason's eyes darkened with emotion. 'Would you have accepted?'

'You know I would.'

Jason bent to bestow a lingering kiss on her mouth. 'Will you marry me now?' he asked softly. 'If you are going to stay, I'd like to get it in writing.'

'Oh, Jason...'

'Well...' He grimaced. 'You've no idea of the hell I've been through since I let you go that first time. I kept telling myself that if we had been married, the situation might never have arisen. And you might have been more prepared to trust me, if I hadn't let you keep your freedom.' He sighed, nuzzling her shoulder. 'What did Irene tell you? Did she reveal the fact that I *was* indirectly responsible for Ridgeway's death, albeit for different reasons.'

'Yes.' Laura spoke honestly. 'She told me every-thing—all about your father, and his arrest, and how he managed to escape imprisonment.' She paused. 'You could have told me, you know. I would never have done anything to hurt you.'

'But you did.' Jason's smile was ironic. 'Again, for the wrong reasons.' He shook his head. 'I wanted to tell you, and I would have done when it was all over, but you took off before I had recovered from the unpleasant after effects of knowing I'd destroyed a man's life!'

'Was that why you...you seemed so withdrawn?'

'I was bitter, I guess. I know I still blamed my father for the mess he had made of my life. But I blamed my-self, too. Even you couldn't change that.'

Laura shook her head. 'If only I'd not jumped to con-clusions...' She gazed up at him. 'But you had been away so much, and when I walked into the Colony Room and saw you with Ellen Ridgeway, I just wanted to die!'

'It wasn't my best moment,' admitted Jason wryly. 'I hated lying to you, and there were times when I wanted to drop the whole thing and give Ridgeway his pound of flesh! But, blackmailers never give up. They just go on, getting more and more greedy, and I couldn't live with that.'

'You know what Ellen said to me, don't you?' mur-mured Laura huskily, delighting in their intimacy. 'I couldn't believe a woman who had just lost her husband would lie to me.'

'Ellen was trying to insure her future,' replied Jason carelessly. 'I guess she realised that Ridgeway's death would make a lot of changes in her life. Not least, financial ones. I had seen her on several occasions, and if you don't think it's too conceited, I'll admit she did make certain…suggestions to me.'

Laura's tongue circled her lips. 'I can imagine.'

'I didn't follow them up,' he declared flatly. 'But while we're having this conversation, I'll explain that that was why I bought the Ridgeway complex.'

Laura's lips quivered. 'As compensation?'

'If you want to put it like that.'

Laura's nails scraped his shoulder. 'What other way is there?'

'Okay.' His expression darkened. 'So now we know why you walked out on me—both times, I guess.' His mouth twisted. 'We hurt one another. I don't want that to happen again.'

'When did you hire a private investigator to watch me?' asked Laura suddenly, and Jason pulled a wry face.

'Would you believe three years ago?' He moved a little restively, and she felt the hard male strength of his body against her thighs. 'Don't ask me why. I guess I had some crazy notion that you might find out and come and see me. I just had to know that you were all right. I even came to London once to see you—to try and convince you I wasn't the bastard you thought I was. But the agent told me you'd found someone else—a man called Carver, with whom you spent more than just office hours. I didn't stay.'

'Oh, darling!' Laura wrapped her arms around him, and pulled him down to her, and for several minutes there was silence in the apartment.

When he finally spoke again, Jason's voice was thick with emotion, his hands possessive as they moved upon her body. 'If you want us to be out of here before tomorrow morning, don't do that again,' he told her unevenly, forcing himself up from her. 'Let me explain how I felt when you came to see me about your sister. I don't want to talk right now but we've got to.' He grunted. 'I never thought I'd have reason to be grateful to Mike Kazantis, but I did.'

'Where is he?' asked Laura frowningly, and Jason sighed.

'I believe he's serving time for fraudulent conversion,' he admitted heavily. 'Now, do you understand why I didn't want you mixed up with that?'

Laura's lips parted. 'He's in prison?'

'For the present,' agreed Jason drily. 'Don't worry. I told Pam the whole story. Like I told you a few weeks ago, your sister is not as fragile as you think.'

'Oh, I know that.' Laura bit her lip. 'She told me if...if I didn't want you, she did.'

Jason groaned. 'That is not my fault.'

'I didn't say it was.' Laura sniffed. 'But I do want you, so I'm afraid she's out of luck.'

'She'll be okay,' said Jason, rolling on to his side and taking her with him. 'When she's had the baby, I'll see she gets a job. And sufficient funds to pay a babyminder, if that's what she wants.'

Laura swallowed. Jason's words about Pamela's baby reminded her of her own disturbing condition, and trailing the tips of her fingers across his chest, she murmured softly, 'Do you really want to marry me?'

'I really do,' he said huskily. 'As soon as it can be arranged.' He frowned. 'You're not changing your mind are you?'

'Oh, no.' Laura spoke fervently. 'I...I just wondered why you...why you took so long to ask me.'

Jason grimaced. 'The truth?'

'Of course.'

'Well, okay. Living with Regina hadn't exactly endeared the institution to me, and I guess I thought I had plenty of time. Then there was Lucy. I thought you didn't think I was such a great father to her, letting her stay with her mother when it was obvious Regina was using her against me. I did think that if we did get married, Lucy could live with us for at least half the time, but it didn't seem fair, loading you with a stepdaughter only eight or nine years younger than you were.'

'Oh, Jason!' Laura gazed at him. 'I love Lucy. You know that. And...and when we are married, I shall want babies.'

'As many as you like,' promised Jason humorously, and Laura sighed.

'Do you mean that?'

'Of course, I mean it.' Jason grimaced. 'Why?'

Laura struggled up into a sitting position and looked down at him with anxious eyes. 'It might be sooner than you think,' she admitted ruefully. 'I was going to call him Jason Huyton, but I suppose Jason Montefiore sounds better.'

Jason jerked her down to him. 'Are you saying— you're pregnant?' He looked stunned. 'Why didn't you tell me?'

'I thought I was doing,' said Laura huskily. 'Do you mind?'

'Mind?' Jason closed his eyes for a moment. Then, opening them again, he fixed her with a penetrating stare. 'You weren't going to tell me, were you? I mean before Irene came to find you.'

'How could I?' Laura pressed her face into the hollow of his neck. 'I didn't want you to think that all I wanted was a father for my child. Afterwards—afterwards, I might have written to you...'

'Written to me?' Jason groaned. 'Oh, love—and I almost sent you away again!'

'But you didn't,' she pointed out softly, and he pressed her closer.

'I couldn't,' he admitted honestly. 'Even though I kept telling myself that all I needed was time, it didn't work before, and I couldn't take the risk. When you walked out of the bedroom, I had to practically drag myself after you. You've no idea how grim I felt when I made it to the door.'

'And now?' she whispered, and he gave her a rueful smile.

'Better—much better,' he conceded roughly. 'How about you?' He drew back to look at her. 'And how do you feel about this baby?'

'*Our* baby?' she murmured, rubbing her chin back and forth against the fine hair on his chest. 'Well—I've had a little longer than you to get used to the idea, and my feelings have never been in doubt.'

'Nor have mine,' declared Jason fiercely, bringing her mouth to his, and Laura knew that this time she had come home.

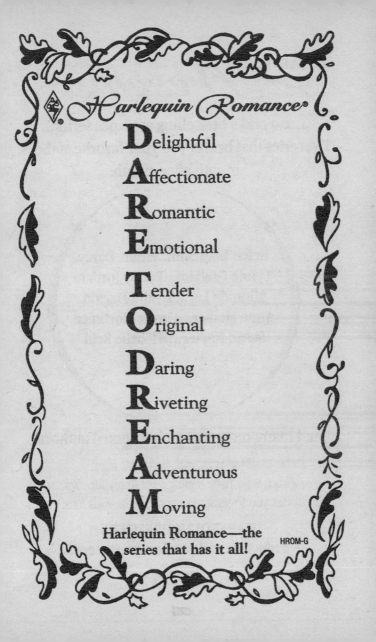

Harlequin Romance®

Delightful

Affectionate

Romantic

Emotional

Tender

Original

Daring

Riveting

Enchanting

Adventurous

Moving

Harlequin Romance—the
series that has it all!

HROM-G

HARLEQUIN *Presents*

**The world's bestselling romance series...
The series that brings you your favorite authors,
month after month:**

Helen Bianchin...Emma Darcy
Lynne Graham...Penny Jordan
Miranda Lee...Sandra Marton
Anne Mather...Carole Mortimer
Susan Napier...Michelle Reid

and many more uniquely talented authors!

Wealthy, powerful, gorgeous men...
Women who have feelings just like your own...
The stories you love, set in exotic, glamorous locations...

**HARLEQUIN PRESENTS,
Seduction and passion guaranteed!**

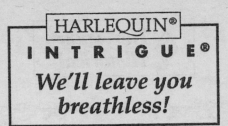

Harlequin® Historical

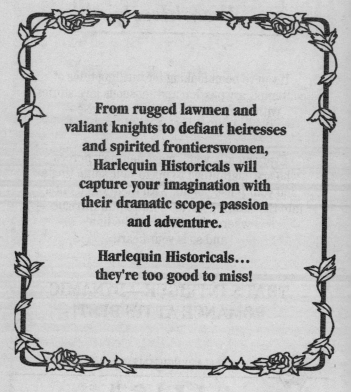

From rugged lawmen and
valiant knights to defiant heiresses
and spirited frontierswomen,
Harlequin Historicals will
capture your imagination with
their dramatic scope, passion
and adventure.

Harlequin Historicals...
they're too good to miss!

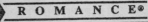

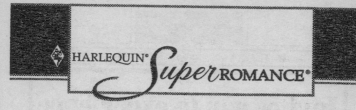

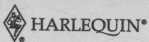